Hello High School

Claire Eaton

Copyright © 2020 Claire Eaton

All rights reserved. No part of this book may be reproduced by any mechanical, photographic, or electronic process, or in the form of a phonographic recording, nor may it be stored in a retrieval system, transmitted, or otherwise be copied for public or private use—other than for "fair use" as brief quotations embodied in articles and reviews without prior written permission of the publisher.

The author of this book does not dispense medical advice nor prescribe the use of any technique as a form of treatment for physical, mental or medical problems without the advice of a physician, either directly or indirectly. The intent of the author is only to offer information of a general nature to help you in your quest for mental fitness and good health. In the event you use any of the information in this book for yourself, the author and the publisher assume no responsibility for your actions.

Published in Australia

Printed in Australia

First Edition

National Library of Australia Cataloguing-in-Publication entry available for this title at nla.gov.au

ISBN: 978-0-6485370-1-4

Cover and Interior Design: Swish Design

I would like to dedicate this book to
every teenager who is showing up, doing your best
and riding the high school rollercoaster with all you've got.

You are awesome!

contents

INTRODUCTION 1

1: Hello SCHOOL ZONE 5

2: Hello HOME ZONE 33

3: Hello PRODUCTIVITY ZONE 57

4: Hello FRIENDSHIP ZONE 97

5: Hello COURAGE ZONE 115

6: Hello MVP ZONE 141

7: Hello SUCCESS ZONE 175

CONCLUSION 187

ACKNOWLEDGEMENTS 189

ABOUT THE AUTHOR 193

INTRODUCTION

Hello high schooler. It's good to meet you!

Or perhaps we've already met—when I have presented at your school, or coached you in my office with Harry my cocker spaniel curled up at your feet. Or maybe you've read *ROC and RISE*—the resilience, optimism and confidence book that helped you level up at school, in your relationships, and in life.

Either way, somehow you've landed yourself a copy of this book. And that's a good thing if you are just starting your high school journey or you are already in Year 8, 9, 10, 11 or 12.

Hello High School is the book you've been waiting for. It has simple and practical answers to all the burning questions asked by high schoolers around the world. Now you can learn what you need, and spend less time worrying and stressing and more time making the most of high school.

It's fair to say that most high schoolers have similar worries, doubts and fears. Which is why this book is jam-packed with more than 85 practical tools, tips and strategies to get you on your way and help you stay on track so you can show up and shine.

Hello High School is divided into seven zones:

1. School
2. Home
3. Productivity
4. Friendship
5. Courage
6. MVP – Most Valuable Player
7. Success

Each zone will deliver the information you need to wipe out your worries and flick away your fears. You can use this book as your handy high school guide, referring to it when you need a question answered or a problem solved.

GOODBYE

Stress, overwhelm, drama, homework hassles, procrastination, worry, and anxiety.

HELLO

Organisation, routine, planning, mindset, friendship, courage, and stepping up to be your best.

This is your zone-by-zone guide to high school. Keep it handy, read it often, and know that your questions are universal (and the answers are somewhere in this book).

SECTION 1

HELLO SCHOOL ZONE
Goodbye needless stress

HELLO SCHOOL ZONE

Being stressed out is revolting. But here's the lowdown: it's normal.

Very, very normal.

It's your body's way of trying to protect you when it detects a 'threat'. And it's been hardwired in our brains since prehistoric times.

You see, back then we had to deal with life-threatening situations (e.g. in prehistoric times, a threat looked like a cheetah chasing us across the savannah) every day. And so our brains and bodies adapted to protect us from these threats in order to stay alive.

At the first sign of danger our brain would pump cortisol (a stress chemical) into our bodies. This chemical would fire up our breathing, muscles and heart so we could fight, freeze on the spot to stay safe, or run for our lives.

Unfortunately, this 'fight or flight' response in our brain is still quite primitive and will often consider situations that might cause stress and anxiety as a 'threat', such as:

- tests and exams
- public speaking
- friendship issues and dramas
- subjects that feel too hard or challenging
- group assignments with new people
- homework overload
- teachers
- rushing between classes when the school is big
- being singled out by a teacher in front of everyone
- telling parents about a stuff-up or poor result.

And before you know it, your body is full of that stress chemical. It's important to remember that while many high school 'threats' are a natural part of life, a stressed brain reacts differently to a chilled brain and can change your behaviour.

WARNING SIGNS

that stress is sticking around and hassling you

CHILLED BRAIN BEHAVIOUR	STRESSED BRAIN BEHAVIOUR
Happy	Moody or snappy
Feeling well and safe	Fierce headaches or sore tummy
Calm heart	Heart pounding in your chest
Feeling you're all sorted	Feeling sensitive and more upset than usual
Learning at a good pace	
Sound sleep	Worried, doubtful thinking
Chilled out	Restless and wide awake
Patient	Tense and uptight
Eating mood-boosting food	Edgy and impatient
Being with friends	Eating food that messes with your mood
Open to new ideas	
Up for a challenge	Hiding in your room

HELLO SCHOOL ZONE

If stress has been sticking to you like glue, I have good news for you. It doesn't need to stay that way.

When stress is moving through your body, head and heart, it's your time to act fast.

You have the power to change it up.

Yes, you do.

Just choose a few strategies from this list of 10 stress-busting moves.

1. EXPECT DIFFICULT DAYS

It can be really annoying when you miss the bus, fail a test, forget your homework, leave your device charger at home, get on the wrong side of a teacher, or get soaked in the rain moving from class to class. Days when everything that can go wrong does go wrong.

Difficult days are normal, temporary and they usually pass. They also make you appreciate the great days so much more.

Here are five things you can do when days are difficult:

1. S-L-O-W DOWN. DO ONE THING AT A TIME.
2. FOCUS ON EVERYTHING THAT IS GOING WELL IN YOUR DAY.
3. CONCENTRATE ON WHAT YOU CAN CONTROL.
4. PAY ATTENTION TO YOUR THOUGHTS. ARE THEY SQUASHING YOU DOWN OR LIFTING YOU UP?
5. BE KIND TO YOURSELF. DIFFICULT DAYS HAPPEN.

2. THINK AGAIN

Don't believe every thought you think.

Why? Because your first thought isn't always your best or your most reliable one.

STRESSFUL THOUGHTS PULL YOU DOWN AND BLOCK YOUR MOOD

"I'll never get this work done in time."

"I won't be selected for the team."

"I bet I fail the next test."

Add your own below:

_____

_____

SOOTHING THOUGHTS PUSH YOU UP AND BOOST YOUR MOOD

"What can I get started on first?"

"I'll do my best to be ready for possible selection."

"I'll work through this test one question at a time."

Add your own here:

_____

_____

How can you turn stressful thoughts into soothing thoughts? Try this simple five-step technique:

1. **CATCH IT** – Notice the thought you are thinking. (Don't be harsh on yourself here.)

2. **CHECK IT** – Is your thought pushing you down or pulling you up?

3. **CHOOSE IT** – If your thought is pushing you down, decide whether you want to keep on the downwards spiral or change it up.

4. **CHANGE IT** – Take a moment to note down a few 'pull up' thoughts on a piece of paper. If you do this enough, it will become easier and more of a natural habit. Soon you won't need to write them down because you'll be able to do them in your head.

5. **REPEAT IT** – Do this again and again, making steps 1-4 your most reliable thinking tool.

Do your best to practise these four steps across all seven zones. With practice you will become better at turning stressful thoughts into soothing ones. And that's a good thing for you, your friends and your family.

> "Just chill and be yourself. It all works out."
> – ALEX

3. TAKE A BREAK

There's a difference between:

GIVING UP	GIVING YOURSELF A BREAK
This is where you pull the pin on something before it's finished, often because you believe it's too hard or challenging. It's where you tell yourself you can't do the task, get a good grade in the assignment, or hand the work in on time.	This is simply where you step away from the challenge for a few minutes because that allows you to take an energy-boosting break. Resting your brain isn't being lazy, (even if it looks like you're not doing anything). When tasks feel tough, taking a break can be a good way to stop, reset and return later.

We all give up sometimes. We are human after all. But if you practise giving up, you'll probably get quite good at giving up. It's a nasty little habit that can make life a bit tricky.

Instead, become a break-taker and you'll master the art of doing the hard thing and discovering how awesome you are.

> "You'll have good and bad days, and that's normal."
> – CHLOE

SOME IDEAS FOR TAKING A BREAK

1.
Cook and create

2.
Jump on the trampoline

3.
Play with your dog

4.
Shoot some hoops

5.
Have a hot shower

6.
Listen to music

7.
Go for a bike ride

4. BE OKAY WITH MAKING MISTAKES

No doubt you'll make tiny and Titanic-sized mistakes at school, in tests, in friendships, on social media, and with teachers.

Mistakes are normal. It's what humans do.

They're not all bad. In fact, some of the coolest things in the world were invented by mistake.

Like fireworks.

Yup, fireworks were a complete scientific accident that hit the world with a bang.

But mistakes can be annoying because they usually mean you didn't get the result you wanted in tests, assignments, sport, or even at home when you're trying to get along with your family.

In the face of mistakes, remind yourself that you're human, dust yourself off, take a deep breath, and feel safe knowing you have two options:

> ⟹ **OPTION 1: REPEAT YOUR MISTAKE = GET THE SAME RESULT.**
>
> Like most people, you've probably tried this already and ended up with nothing but a bucketload of frustration.
>
> ⟹ **OPTION 2: LEARN FROM YOUR MISTAKE = GIVE YOURSELF A BETTER CHANCE OF GETTING A DIFFERENT RESULT.**
>
> This takes work, but will increase your chance of getting a bucketload of knowledge, wisdom, and high school happiness.

When mistakes pop up, and you want to learn from them and give yourself the best chance of getting a different result in the future, try these tactics:

☆ THINK ONE KIND AND REMINDING THOUGHT ☆

I am not my mistake. I'm a good person who is learning my way through high school and that's okay.

Ask Six Curious Questions

1. Do I need to say sorry or check whether someone is okay?
2. What didn't go to plan?
3. What could I do differently or change next time?
4. Do I need help to make this change?
5. How will I know my changes or new plans are working?
6. Do I need to accept I made a mistake and forgive myself?

Here's another little secret about making mistakes. Your family love you to the moon and back, and that will not change because you stuffed up. Even if they give you a serve when you spill the beans about your mistake, they still love you.

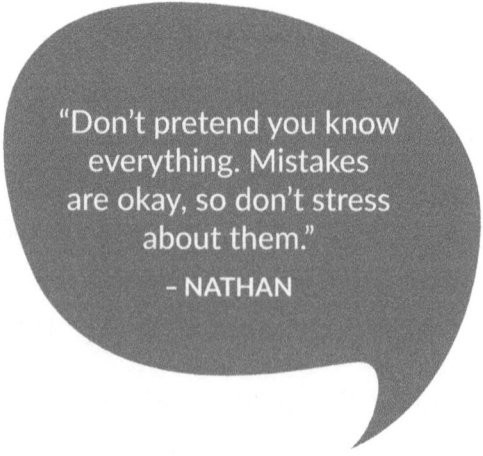

"Don't pretend you know everything. Mistakes are okay, so don't stress about them."
– NATHAN

5. PUSH BACK ON PERFECTIONISM

Perfectionism is often cleverly disguised as 'trying hard' and 'doing your best'. But it's actually aiming beyond your personal best, which can bring on anxiety, overwhelm, and feelings of panic and doubt.

Have you ever:

- had a test handed back and felt your heart sink because your score wasn't 'perfect' enough?
- played for your team and missed a few shots?
- spoken at assembly and stumbled over your words?
- baked cupcakes that didn't rise to perfection?

Don't be fooled into thinking being perfect in maths, science, English or sport will bring you high school happiness or increased popularity. That's a crazy, wild and far-fetched myth.

> "Success and failure are a part of life. I've done both heaps of times, and it all worked out fine."
> – KELLIE

WHAT'S HELPFUL	WHAT'S UNHELPFUL
You

Showing up

Focusing on ongoing success and achievements

Accepting yourself on your good, bad, and in-between days

Giving yourself and others permission to be perfectly imperfect | Competing with yourself and everyone else to achieve the perfect:

body and personality

height and weight

hair and skin

score and result

friendship |

KICK PERFECTION TO THE CURB

Life happens. Things go right,
and things go wrong.

Don't waste your time putting yourself down.

Do remember that you're human,
and you're all good.

THERE'S NO BETTER TIME THAN NOW

Waiting for the perfect time is like waiting for the stars, moon, sun and clouds to align. Waiting can paralyse your thinking and dull your spark. You get yourself stuck and end up doing absolutely nothing.

What if right now is the perfect time to make your move? What if right now is the time to stop waiting and start doing?

Join the club. Now.

Eat the cake. Now.

Go on the camp. Now.

Say "Yes". Now.

Say "No". Now.

Put your hand up and ask the question. Now.

Finish the assignment and hand it in. Now.

Speak face to face. Now.

Talk about the problem. Now.

Borrow a board and learn to surf. Now.

Do the dance. Now.

Audition for the school production. Now.

6. SEARCH FOR SOLUTIONS

Problems pop up in life. At school. In sport. In friendships and family. With teachers, the weather, teammates, food, clothes, parties …

And the list goes on.

'Problem pushing' is an easy habit to fall into. But the good news is it's a habit you can change.

You know you're problem pushing when you:

- hear yourself talking negatively about teachers
- retell stories about losing and failing in sport
- get involved in other people's problems
- reject ideas from parents that could help solve a problem
- refuse to listen to fresh and helpful ideas
- find yourself surrounded by other problem pushers
- don't feel great because your heart and head are stuck in life's problems.

If this sounds like you, and you want to change it up, you need to …

— draw a line in the sand —

… and then:

1. **PAY ATTENTION TO YOUR THOUGHTS.**
   (This doesn't mean get bogged down in them. It simply means being aware of what's running through your mind.)

2. **PUT YOUR PROBLEMS IN THE PAST.**
   (This doesn't mean pretending they don't exist. It simply means being brave and shifting your thinking away from 'doom and gloom' that can flatten your mood.)

3. **SET SOLUTIONS FOR THE FUTURE.**
   (This doesn't mean believing there's a perfect solution for everything in life. It means being brave and choosing to be curious and 'forward thinking' to boost your mood.)

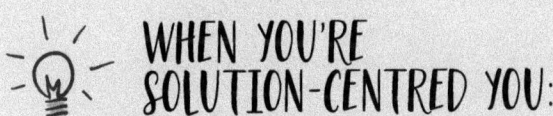

WHEN YOU'RE SOLUTION-CENTRED YOU:

- spend time with people who talk about solutions and good news
- visualise images of situations ending well in your mind
- direct conversations towards new ideas and positivity
- ask, "What can I do to make a difference?"
- ask, "What needs to improve to get a better result?"

There are no guarantees in life. But by practising solution-centred habits you'll be spending more time on the lighter, brighter side of that line in the sand.

And that's got to be a good thing.

NOTE: If you notice you're getting good at this solution-centred thinking, good on you. You should be proud of yourself. But don't go around telling other people how to do things and insist they follow your lead. That would be annoying. Instead, keep being a solution-centred human. Other people will see you, hear you, and get a good feeling around you. And pretty soon then they may want to join your party. But that will be their choice.

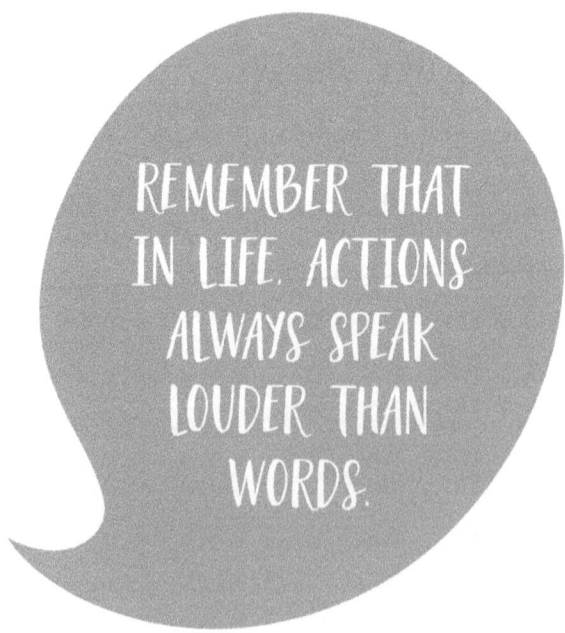

REMEMBER THAT IN LIFE, ACTIONS ALWAYS SPEAK LOUDER THAN WORDS.

7. TUNE IN TO TEACHERS

It's easy to make snap judgements about teachers. They can stress you out, and make you love or loathe a subject at school.

But remember: **first impressions are not always right.**

Here are FIVE WAYS snap judgements can hold you back

1. Deciding you're not a fan of your teacher's vibe and you never will be.
2. Tricking yourself into believing a subject is extra hard or boring because you don't like the teacher.
3. Showing up to class with less energy and a bad attitude.
4. Talking about the teacher behind their back.
5. Giving up in class because you don't warm to your teacher or their style.

Here are FIVE TIPS to get you back on track

1. Keep your teacher and the subject separate.
2. Look for your teacher helping someone and showing patience in tricky situations.
3. Consider judging your teacher less and accepting them more.
4. Acknowledge what you appreciate and are grateful for in their class.
5. Check you are proud of your energy and attitude. If not, is there room for change?

> "It's okay if your opinion about school and teachers change."
> – ZANE

8. TURN CRITICISM INTO FEEDBACK

Teachers want you to shine. And from time to time they'll tell you how you're going.

It can be easy to confuse feedback and criticism. But there's a big difference.

Criticism is stuck in the past. It:

- feels cold and a bit judgy
- focuses on the mistakes and stuff-ups you made
- talks a lot about previous scores and results
- leaves you feeling stuck.

Criticism can make a lot of people become super sensitive and defensive because they think they're being picked on.

Feedback is looking into the future. It:

- feels friendly and kind
- helps you see where you can improve
- talks about ways to learn from mistakes
- encourages you to dust yourself off and move forward.

When you take something on as feedback, you know you're being helped by someone who cares about you. And when you're helping a friend or classmate, make sure you're giving them feedback too. They will definitely appreciate it.

GET CURIOUS, NOT FURIOUS

Try turning criticism into feedback.

Ignore the harsh way something may have been delivered, and pay attention only to the facts you hear. If they're valuable, use them to make a change. If they're not, wave them goodbye.

9. DON'T LET BOREDOM GET THE BEST OF YOU

At school you will feel bored at some point. That's to be expected. Not everything in school (or life for that matter) is going to raise the roof with excitement.

But boredom and daydreaming can crank up your creativity and even reveal your next BIG IDEA.

Remember me talking about fireworks being the result of a mistake? Well they were the result of boredom too. Two thousand years ago a cook in China packed charcoal, saltpetre and sulphur into a bamboo tube, which then exploded when he set it alight.

BOREDOM CAN BE POWERFUL.

Maybe the subject doesn't interest you. Maybe the work is too easy or too hard, and you've lost interest. I bet you experienced the same thing in primary school.

But here's the thing. In primary school you had one, maybe two teachers who knew you pretty well during the year. And because they knew you so well, they could remind, prompt and even reward you for pushing on and getting the job done—even when you were bored.

It's different in high school. You have half a dozen or more teachers who see you only a couple of times a week. So chances are they'll never know you as well as your primary school teachers did, and may not be able to push you as much as they did either.

Which means you need to learn to push yourself.

So the next time boredom strikes:

1. ASK FOR HELP

Can your teacher or desk partner help you out? Your teacher may have a preferred 'help' system set up for you to use when you feel stuck. Don't hold back. Work completion beats boredom, and also reduces the amount of work you have to do after school.

2. DIG DEEPER

Search for questions and tasks you *do* understand and dive into them. This relieves boredom, and helps you get closer to finishing the job. And finishing is a great feeling.

10. LET LAUGHTER IN

High school doesn't have to be so serious. Seriously, it doesn't.

You'll make mistakes and feel so embarrassed. Your face will be glowing red, and you'll want the ground to open up and swallow you.

Yup, that's normal.

So join the 'I make a fool of myself sometimes' club, which recommends you practise:

- finding funny moments in stressful times
- laughing at yourself until your belly hurts.

WHY LAUGH?

You feel more connected to your friends when you laugh together.

It pumps 'feel good' chemicals (endorphins) into your body, and lowers the stress chemical (cortisol) levels in your body.

Your immune system also gets a boost, which is great if you want to feel happy and healthy.

> "Don't be the fun police. Laugh at yourself and make school happy."
> – GABBY

SECTION 2

HELLO HOME ZONE

Goodbye homework hassle

HELLO HOME ZONE

You probably know why doing schoolwork, assignments and study at home messes with your head. But in case you think you're the only person who feels that way, here's what other teens say about doing schoolwork at home:

- "I'm not that interested."
- "I feel stressed and overwhelmed."
- "I get off the bus late and I'm tired."
- "I have heaps of sport commitments."
- "I want to hang with my friends."
- "I'm over it. So over it."
- "It causes arguments in our family."
- "I have a part-time job after school."
- "I'd rather be doing things I enjoy when I get home."

As you can see, you're not alone. But (and there's always a 'but', right?) doing schoolwork at home is part of the high school journey. It may not always be filled with fun and excitement but that's the way it is.

10 STRATEGIES
for effectively managing homework and study

1. CREATE A 'FINISH OFF' FOLDER

If you're in class and your teacher says, "If you haven't finished yet, please finish it off at home", add that work to your 'finish off' folder. It's now your top priority—the first thing you do when you start your homework session.

Why? Because it's easy to lose track of unfinished work. And too much unfinished work can weigh on your mind and create extra stress you don't need.

The work in your 'finish off' folder should be fresh in your mind, which will make it easier to get it done and ready to hand in. Don't put it aside until later. Get it done first.

2. SET YOURSELF UP FOR SUCCESS

Here are three simple things you can do to boost your chances of being effective with the work you do at home.

1. BE DIARY SMART

Got any homework, assignments, or study that needs to be done? Put it in your diary, along with clear instructions so you'll know exactly what you need to do when you get home. Something like this:

> Page 30: answer questions 9-11.
>
> Chapter 10: highlight eight keywords.
>
> Finish maths sheet.

Don't try to store everything in your head. Your brain can't cope, and you run the risk of having a meltdown because your head feels so full, heavy and cluttered.

Sound familiar?

2. BE CLASS SMART

If your teacher's rule is that unfinished classwork becomes homework, make a note to use your class time wisely. Chat less and work more during class time so you have less work to take home and, more time to do the things you love.

Makes sense, right?

3. BE FUEL SMART

Before you try to use your brain after school, fill your belly with good food. Take a break when you get home, and eat, drink and chill out before you hit your homework. You'll be amazed how much a half-hour break can help you become more productive when you need to be.

3. CHIP AWAY WITH DAILY REVISION

What's revision? It's looking back over the work you did at school that day or in the previous few days.

Revision might mean:

- reading notes
- doing practice questions
- watching information videos
- highlighting key points on examples
- discussing topics with friends.

Why revise? It allows you to check your understanding.

- Does this idea or formula make sense?
- If it doesn't, what's the information gap you need help to close?
- What help do you need to close that gap?

Once you know you need help, you can:

- email your teacher
- ask a question the next day in class
- do a Google search
- ask a friend in a group chat
- check in with your parent.

The important thing is to not leave that information gap open. If you do, it will cause you stress when you get ready to study and your mind is totally blank. Learn as you go rather than trying to cram it all into your study time.

TOP TIP

Revising each day is a great way to stay up to date and be prepared when you start studying for texts and exams.

4. CREATE SOUND STUDY PRACTICES

Study is going back over what you've already learned so you can be tested in exam conditions. It's a good idea to experiment to find out your study preference and what works best for you.

IF YOU'RE A TALKER

1. Create question cards, and ask someone to test you. Put the answers on the back so they know whether you're on the right track with your answers.
2. Set a timer for one to three minutes. Keep talking about the subject until the timer sounds. If you run out of words, that might be a clue that you need to gather more information.

IF YOU'RE A LISTENER

1. Record yourself answering questions on a device and play it back. Use a self-made checklist so you know whether you've hit your target.
2. Listen to podcasts and take notes while you listen.

IF YOU'RE A READER

1. Highlight your notes.
2. Read chapters in books.
3. Read examples of answers completed in previous years.

IF YOU'RE A WRITER

1. Write down the answers to tests.
2. Write a list of important facts, and then expand on each one.
3. Write flashcards.

IF YOU'RE A THINKER

1. Gather questions that take your knowledge to the next level.
2. Brainstorm what you know about each topic.
3. Create mind maps to show your knowledge.

IF YOU'RE A CONNECTOR

1. Meet with friends to discuss ideas and test each other.
2. Create five questions, ask your friends to do the same, and then swap. You can even mark them together to double up on learning.
3. Watch videos and information shows with like-minded learners.

5. DO A SUNDAY SETUP SESSION

If you're feeling overwhelmed and stressed, and freaking out about all your homework, assignments and study, see whether a regular Sunday setup session can get you back on track.

Here's how:

1. Block out a chunk of time on Sunday (or Saturday—either day will work).
2. Make sure you have:
    - a diary, planner, whiteboard or your smart phone
    - dates for all the meetings, tests and work you need to complete in each subject
    - your sport, music, drama and tutor days and times.
3. Order the dates from soonest to latest, and put them all in your diary.
4. Crunch the numbers. Estimate how much time you will need to complete each task.
5. Chunk your homework or study down into weekly and then daily tasks.

This will allow you to stop talking about what's not working, and encourage you to start looking at what is working, so you can do more of it.

It will also help you to stop making promises you know you can't deliver on just to make someone:

- like you
- invite you
- include you
- approve of you
- be kind to you.

Sunday setup sessions will help you get clear about what is right for you.

6. PRACTISE PRIORITISING

Do you jump from task to task, leaving a trail of unfinished work behind you?

"HELLO STRESS!"

Does it feel like assignments and homework keep piling up?

"HELLO PANIC!"

Is your to-do list so chock-a-block that you don't know where to start, and so you don't at all?

"HELLO WORRY!"

If you answered "Yes" to these questions, it's okay. It happens to most people at some stage during high school.

When you find yourself in this spot it's time to hit:

STOP
on the panic,
stress and worry
buttons.

START
on the
TAKE ACTION
button.

It's time to start prioritising. If you don't take action (i.e. do something different to what you're doing now) nothing will change. Netflix, gaming, couch surfing and hoping things will get better won't make things better.

But action will.

And the best kind of action here is to prioritise: decide what is most important in your life right now, and then schedule time to do it.

If you practise prioritising you will feel less overwhelmed, anxious and guilty when you haven't done everything at home or at school that you think you should have.

7. REMEMBER THAT COMPLETION BEATS PERFECTION

Some parts of high school may feel like a never-ending loop.

1. Start the task.
2. Do the work.
3. Complete it.
4. Hand it in on time.
5. Get a score.
6. Move on to the next task, test, assignment or exam.
7. Repeat.

Just like tidying your room and doing the dishes, the loop continues. (And so do the eye rolls.)

If you get hooked into unrealistic thinking (e.g. this task must be 100% picture perfect and absolutely award winning so the teacher will think I'm incredible, people will like me more, and my parents will tell me I'm amazing), you'll quickly run out of puff (not to mention time).

Why? Because you'll constantly get stuck on Steps three and four.

Think about it. If you never complete a task because you're trying so hard to perfect it, you'll get lost in the loop and fall further behind.

You're a human being. And that means you sometimes need to be with friends and family, playing sport, exercising, doing things you love, or just hanging around not doing much. Don't underestimate the benefits of chill out time, and don't allow perfectionism to squeeze these simple joys out of your life.

Instead, abide by these three simple rules and mantras:

1. DON'T WAIT FOR THE PERFECT MOMENT BECAUSE THE PERFECT MOMENT IS NOW.

2. DON'T LET PERFECTION GET IN THE WAY OF COMPLETION.

3. PROGRESS WILL ALWAYS BEAT PERFECTION.

8. TAKE BRAIN AND BODY BREAKS

Your brain likes things that are new and interesting. That's why it's important to give it a break when it starts getting bored or worn out from learning.

Everyone is different. But if you pay attention, you'll notice that your brain and body have a tipping point. They give you signals you need to take break, such as:

- becoming restless and fidgety
- becoming distracted by devices, food, games, messages, and even the most mundane things
- re-reading what you just read because you've already forgotten what it was about
- slouching, yawning and doing nothing
- making more mistakes than usual
- finding that nothing makes sense, and you are feeling really confused.

What should you do when your brain is giving you these signals?

Take a break.

What kind of break do you need? Chances are you'll need either a 'wake up' break or 'wind down' break.

THE 'WAKE UP' BREAK

If you've been doing the same thing for a while, you might need a 'wake up' break.

'Wake up' breaks stimulate you, fire you up, and give you fresh energy so that when you get back to the task at hand you have more energy to get it done.

You just need to choose a 'wake up' that works for you. For example, you could:

- whip up a delight in the kitchen
- listen to loud music
- flip on the trampoline
- kick the footy
- play with your dog
- switch to a hobby you love.

Whatever you choose, make sure it brings you joy and wakes you up.

THE 'WIND DOWN' BREAK

If you've been in high energy mode for a while and your brain has been working overtime, it will be screaming at you to switch to a pace that's a bit more chilled. A 'wind down' break brings calm so you can get back to the task feeling more settled and get it done.

For your 'wind down' activity you could:

- chill on the couch
- watch Netflix
- chat with your family at the kitchen bench
- edit some photos
- cook
- cuddle with your dog
- watch your favourite sports team on TV.

Just make sure that what you choose brings calm to your mind.

9. BE EXAM AWARE

Tests and exams are not designed to stress you out. Rather, they're a way for you and your teachers to get a clear idea of:

- what you know and understand in each subject
- where you need help or extra support
- what you're AWESOME at. (Do you pump out bigger scores in certain subjects? This could be a clue as to what career path you may be leaning towards.)

Here are some awesome exam tips and tricks that will help you get through in good shape.

BEFORE AN EXAM

- Avoid conversations that squash your confidence. You need your mojo. Hang on tight.
- Avoid people who are panicking and trying to pull you into a thinking mess. Step away. Panic is a pest.
- Avoid questions like "Did you study [insert topic]?" This is an energy-draining trap.

DURING AN EXAM

- Breathe. Take slow, deep, calming, beautiful breaths. Let the oxygen flow around your body so you don't become a tangled mess.

- Read one question and answer it, and then move on to the next. Or read all the questions and choose which you want to start on first. (It's okay to answer questions out of order.) You'll see which approach works best for you. If one option creates an ugly feeling inside you, choose the other option instead.

- Resist the temptation to look at people around you. How they approach things is not your business, nor is the time they finish. If they leave early, stretch in their chair, or look like they're totally nailing this test, repeat to yourself, *not my business, I am doing my best.*

AFTER AN EXAM

- Avoid conversations that make you doubt your performance.

- Wind down to charge up. If you need to play with your dog, do that. Maybe you want to eat tasty toasties and watch Netflix, or hang out with friends and swim in the pool. Whatever does the job, go and do it.

- Avoid questions like "Did you write this?" and "Did you include that?" because these can go one of two ways:
    1. "Yes, I did." (Whoop whoop!)
    2. "No, I didn't." (OMG. I failed.)

10. CALL ON PARENT POWER

Your parents want to help you, especially during your high school years. So do your grandparents, your aunties, your uncles, your stepparents, your carers, and the house mums and dads at your boarding school.

But here's the thing: these adults can't help you if they don't know you need help.

If you feel stuck or out of your depth, and you need something but aren't sure what it is exactly, these ideas might be useful. Let your parent know which one you need, and watch them work their magic.

- A good old pep talk to boost you up if you're feeling low.
- A hug to make you feel supported and nurtured.
- Fresh ideas, especially if you've hit your tipping point and your brain is bursting.
- Help to understand the task. (They may not know the answer, but they can work with you to help you find it.)
- Time alone. (Let your parent know everything is okay, and that you just need to chill.)
- A chat with your teacher to 'reset' and get back on track.
- Family fun—time with those you love the most.
- Time with your friends if you're missing them.

SECTION 3

HELLO PRODUCTIVITY ZONE

Goodbye procrastination and overwhelm

HELLO PRODUCTIVITY ZONE

What's procrastination? It's the fancy word for ignoring and delaying tasks until 'later', or allowing yourself to be easily distracted.

Here's the slippery slope procrastination takes us down.

STEP 1 - YOU PUT THINGS OFF AGAIN AND AGAIN

Why? Perhaps the work is too hard or too boring, you're not interested, or you don't want to do the work unless you can do it perfectly.

STEP 2 - YOU DO FUN THINGS INSTEAD OF GETTING THE JOB DONE

Let's face it: watching Netflix is a lot more fun than doing that assignment. Your brain likes fun stuff, remember? Every time you do fun stuff, your brain is rewarded with a hit of dopamine—a happy hormone that makes you feel good. So good in fact, that it sends you on a mission looking for more Netflix, skateboarding, social scrolling, gaming, shopping, and hanging with your friends. Dopamine makes it easy to put off the jobs that need doing until 'later'.

STEP 3 - YOU GET STRESSED OUT

Unfortunately, 'later' usually arrives at 10pm the night before the work is due. Stress, worry and anxiety come out to play, because now the pressure is on. Does this sound familiar? You are now forced to act fast; find a way to complete the work, wing it, or come up with an excuse to escape doing it. And none of those options sound like they would end well.

STEP 4 - PARENTS AND TEACHERS NAG YOU

Why? Because procrastination looks a lot like laziness. Arguments start and detentions are given because your parents and teachers think you're being lazy, disorganised and dodging your responsibilities.

Which may be the truth sometimes. But it doesn't have to be this way.

HOW DO YOU KNOW PROCRASTINATION IS BLOCKING YOU?

- You're constantly switching from task to task.
- You pull out when work gets tough.
- You start tasks way too late creating crazy deadlines for yourself.
- You're constantly stressing about work, but not getting it done.
- You feel far too rushed and under the pump.
- Your workstation is messy.
- You make plans but forget them.
- You get distracted by all the fun things in life.

HOW DO YOU BEAT PROCRASTINATION? WITH THESE ...

10 WAYS
to get work done on time

1. STOP RELYING ON MOTIVATION

Move over motivation, you're totally overrated. Routine is here to shake things up!

Routines are reliable. *Motivation is not.*

If you get stuck in the procrastination trap, routines will help you. *Motivation will not.*

If you feel overwhelmed at school or at home, routines are your friend. *Motivation is not.*

If your timetable is jam-packed with school, sport and social events, routine is your go-to. *Motivation is not.*

What are routines? They're sets of actions you choose to repeat. Routines make your brain happier as it switches to autopilot, creating a helpful habit loop.

Routines can be super simple:

- showering first thing in the morning, or maybe just before bed
- drizzling a spoonful of honey on your favourite cereal
- charging your devices at the same time every day
- brushing your teeth without giving it a second thought

That's routine doing its thing, and priming you for less stress and more success at home and at school.

Routines stand up when motivation falls.

Your daily high school routine might look like this:

- Morning music playlist, shower, breakfast, make your bed, get dressed and be ready before your 7.40am departure to catch the bus. Your bag is at the door because you put it there the night before.
- Arrive at school, sort your locker out so you're set for the first two classes, then chat with friends until the bell sounds.
- Get home and eat, chill out for a bit before your 5pm phone reminder to finish off your work and do revision. Even your dog knows the drill, snuggling at your feet every afternoon.

ARE YOU ROUTINE READY?

Note down some routines you can add to your day or week:

⇓ **SPEND LESS TIME**
trying to motivate yourself to get homework, study and assignments done.

⇑ **SPEND MORE TIME**
following well-set routines so your homework, revision, study and assignments get done and submitted on time.

And here's the bonus: routines give you more time to do fun stuff. When your essays are done and dusted, you can hit the surf without the stress of thinking *I should be doing my assignment*. (It also gets your parents off your back.)

You get the satisfaction of completing the assignment and the boost of being able to get out and enjoy life stress-free. That's a double dose of dopamine right there.

Who doesn't want more of that?

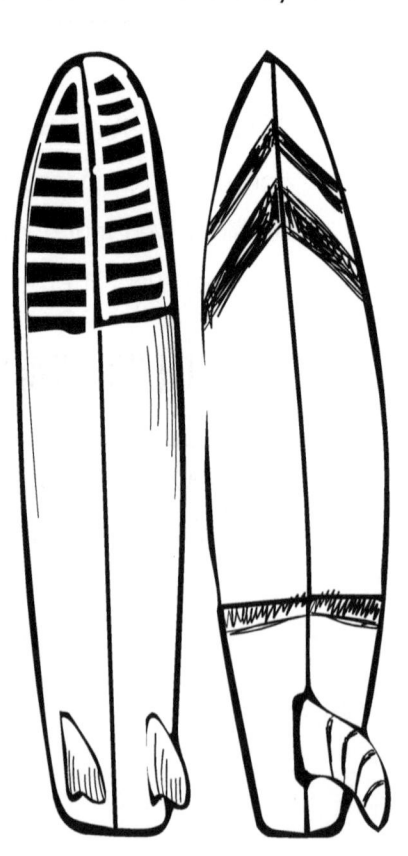

2. CLEAR THE CLUTTER

Humans love anything that makes life easier and less stressful (such as creating routines). But sometimes we make our lives harder by surrounding ourselves with clutter.

Weird, right?

Cluttered areas can overwhelm your brain, making it harder to think clearly, make plans and smash goals. In contrast, clutter-free areas soothe your brain so you can study or finish your homework with fewer distractions.

If clutter is piling up on the floor, your desk, or sneaking out of your cupboard onto your bed, you need to put a clutter-free system in place.

GOODBYE CLUTTER

All your clothes, shoes, books, devices, makeup, sports gear, files and notes need a permanent place to call home. If they don't have a home, they usually find their own.

That's how clutter rolls, so get your hands on:

- stackable storage boxes and baskets
- labels, hooks and pinboards
- desk organisers and drawer dividers.

These are all game-changers.

HELLO SYSTEMS

Labelled boxes, divided drawers, hooks and ordered shelves will give your stuff a home. You'll now be able to put things away after you've finished using them.

Sounds like a brilliant plan, right?

INCLUDE TECHNOLOGY

You should also:

- delete apps you're no longer using
- sort the files and folders on your computer's desktop
- box up your old cables and chargers
- decide whether your online groups are still for you.

Note: if clearing away clutter isn't your favourite thing to do, you may not get the hit of dopamine you were hoping for. But keep going, because dopamine loves a grand final party. You'll get a mighty hit of it when you can finally stand back, admire your work, and feel on top of things.

If you're wondering where to start, here are some handy rules for clutter:

- "I use this every day."

    Keep it handy on your workstation.

- "I use this a lot."

    Make sure it's always within easy reach.

- "I don't use this much."

    Label it and store it away.

- "I never use this."

    Do you still need it? If not, can you pay it forward, recycle it, or sell it for extra cash?

HELLO PRODUCTIVITY ZONE

3. SET UP YOUR WORKSTATION

Find a place, claim your space, and make it your own.

Your workstation needs to be set up well. If it's a nice place to work you'll feel more confident and comfortable doing homework, studying for tests, and coming up with cool ideas.

And it's especially important if frustration, boredom or confusion are trying to sneak in and stop you from pushing through to the end of a task.

10 TOP WORKSTATION SETUP TIPS

1. Keep your desk clear of distractions. You want to place non-essential devices far away from your workstation, so you're less tempted to check messages and watch hilarious YouTube videos.

2. Check you have good light, fresh air, and a chair with good support. Resist the temptation to study on your bed. It isn't great for your posture or motivation and let's face it: a sneaky 10-minute snooze or quick Netflix session is hard to resist.

3. Surround yourself with motivating pictures and inspiring quotes to keep you productive when you can't be bothered anymore.

4. If you work best at the dining table and prefer having people around you, you can still set up and pack up your workstation each time. Consider having a box or basket to hold all your gear, and then set it up and pack it up as part of your homework routine.

5. Experiment with essential oil diffusers. Peppermint oil is good to spike your attention, and lavender is great if you're looking to calm your mind.

6. Noise-cancelling headphones can be handy if you have younger siblings in the house or need silence to stay in the zone.

7. Sticky notes, pinboards and whiteboards help you stay organised.

8. Blue light glasses are awesome. They filter blue light and reduce glare.

9. Pot plants at your workstation can help improve air quality and reduce stress. A peace lily plant is a low maintenance goodie.

10. Many teens say a stand-up converter for your desk, or a large inflatable fit ball are great ways to change it up when doing longer study stints.

4. WORK OUT YOUR WHY

Chances are some parts of school won't exactly float your boat. And to get through them you'll need to take a big breath, dig deep, and look beyond the worksheet you're doing or exam that's looming.

By looking forward you can work out your WHY, your personal reason for pushing through when you don't want to.

When you do this, it can help you notice if your thoughts are holding you back or moving you forward:

- HOLDING THOUGHTS – hold your focus on **the task** you dislike and reasons not to do it.

- MOVING THOUGHTS – direct your focus towards **the outcome** you would like and reasons to get it done.

Here are some examples from high schoolers just like you:

JANE - YEAR 9

HOLDING THOUGHT: I'm not interested in comparing two cartoons in English and having to answer a zillion questions about them. What's the point? Why am I spending my time doing this?

MOVING THOUGHT: I want to hand it in, hopefully pass, and give myself a chance to get the best grade I can on my next report. That's my WHY.

MAX - YEAR 10

HOLDING THOUGHT: Having to do sport four times a week is so annoying, especially as I'm not very sporty. I don't get it. Why do I have to show up to do something I don't like? I'm not that good at it either.

MOVING THOUGHT: I still need to exercise at school. I don't play sport, but I want to stay as fit and healthy as I can and exercise with my mates. That's my WHY.

ELLIE - YEAR 8

HOLDING THOUGHT: Maths is so boring. It's hard, and I don't want to do it. Why do I have to finish this?

MOVING THOUGHT: I want to get this done and handed in because it's better being up to date than falling behind. That's my WHY.

TOP TIP

Make a WHY sign and keep it in front of you at your workstation.

When you're doing work that isn't floating your boat and you notice you're thinking too many holding thoughts, use moving thoughts to remind you to push on.

Your why is waiting—stay fit and exercise with your mates, get the grade you want on your report, or be up to date in maths.

5. USE CLOCKS AND TIMERS

When you're at your workstation, you need to train your brain to concentrate for long periods of time. At school your teachers do this for you with reminders and prompts, but at home you need to be your own boss and manage your own time.

Using timers can help you concentrate, stay on task, and push back on procrastination.

Depending on your age and experience with timers, you may want to start small (five to ten minutes). But over weeks and months keep extending the duration until you can concentrate at your workstation for 40–60 minutes without any problems.

Why? Because by the time you reach the senior years of high school, you'll be sitting tests and exams that can go on for two or three hours. And if you're struggling to focus, that time can slip away very quickly. So start training your brain now, and keep extending that timeframe. You won't regret it.

> **TOP TIP**
> *It's natural for your attention span to feel different depending on your mood, the day of the week, and whether or not you're tired. Go with the flow, and remember that you just need to do your best because your best is enough.*

6. HAVE FEWER LATE NIGHTS

Here's the low-down on last-minute late nights:

THE PAIN	THE PLEASURE
You're stressed out. Anxiety takes over. Your parents are on your back. Your brain is overloaded and hurting. Waking up the next morning is a struggle. You're exhausted at school the next day. Your work might not be up to scratch. You catch yourself taking shortcuts. You start making mistakes. You regret staying up late, and wish you'd started the work sooner.	Zero

Nobody is perfect. Late nights happen. But you shouldn't be having them consistently and frequently. They won't help you to feel good or reach your potential.

7. DOMINATE YOUR DEVICES

Do your devices dominate you, your mood, and how much work you get done?

If you're nodding in agreement, it's time to turn the tables and become a device dominator:

THUMBS DOWN
You're getting sucked into checking messages + watching videos while doing homework = unhappy brain and time wasted being unproductive (and taking longer than needed to get the job done).

THUMBS UP
- Silence your phone or put it in another room.
- Activate aeroplane mode.
- Turn off notifications on devices you're using to get the work done.

DID YOU KNOW

When your device sucks you in and you're distracted, it can take your brain up to five minutes to refocus on the original task. If you check your phone five times in an hour-long study session, you could lose up to 25 minutes of quality study time.

Life's too precious for that!

8. DO THE WORK

People tend to approach their desire to achieve and succeed in high school in one of two ways.

METHOD 1 - MAGIC

Believing they will magically and easily succeed with no setbacks along the way. They just wish and wait for their work to be done for them.

METHOD 2 - WORK AND GRIT

Knowing they are the one who must dig deep, push past challenges, and do the work to stay in the zone. They ask for help if they need it, and celebrate little wins along the way because they deserve it.

Give both methods a go and you'll soon work out that:

- The homework fairy will not rescue you when the magic doesn't happen, and you'll need to pull an all-nighter.
- The more you practise 'working', the better you become at 'working'.

> "Take every opportunity to see what you can achieve."
> – TAHLIA

9. REWARD YOURSELF

There's nothing wrong with giving yourself a pat on the back when you achieve your goal. In fact, it's an awesome habit to get into.

But be careful. Things can get messy if you always have your eye on rewards that are super fancy, cost heaps of money, or are out of your league. Clothes, devices, parties and gifts of money all have the potential to pull you away from your WHY and push you towards fake and short-term 'happy face' rewards.

Feelings and emotions such as pride and joy pour from your heart when you know deep inside that you've done something good. (Dopamine shows up once again.)

Keep it simple. 'Inside' rewards are the best, such as:

- sleeping in
- sharing great news with your family or a close friend
- making a Milo and watching Netflix
- going for a swim at the beach
- treating yourself to a slice of your favourite cake
- hanging out with your besties
- shooting hoops after school.

10. TELL YOUR FRIENDS YOU'RE ON A MISSION

Your friends want to hang out and chat with you. Of course they do. But sometimes you'll need to step up and let them know that you're on a mission, and need to bunker down and plough through your to-do list.

In summary, you're asking your friends to support you 100% by messaging you less, not messaging at all, or holding off until you message them first.

You should also ask them not to tag you in fun photos on the socials, or send videos of their awesome time at the beach or links to YouTube funnies (the ultimate distractors).

Sometimes it's easier to get on with your work when you don't know what all your friends are doing while you are studying. Being honest with your friends and telling them how it is will work in your favour. You'll all start to understand and appreciate that there are times for fun and games and times to knuckle down and get the work done (which is pretty much what life is all about).

And it can be a great opportunity to make plans to catch up when your work is all done and dusted—that's a nice reward for you all to look forward to.

Telling your friends about your 'get work done' mission will help you beat procrastination and overwhelm, and stay in the productivity zone.

Now let's talk about OVERWHELM

Breathe a sigh of relief. Overwhelm is normal, and everyone feels it from time to time.

Life can be super-speed busy from the moment you wake up until the moment your head hits the pillow. And some days (or even weeks) in high school can be more chaotic than others, especially if you're involved in a few groups, clubs and teams.

With this in mind, do your best to get through the busier times and keep reminding yourself that you're only human.

But there's a limit to the amount of overwhelm your head, heart and body can handle. You've probably worked this out already.

WARNING SIGNS
that overwhelm is taking over your day

The good news is you can beat overwhelm if you're willing to drill down and explore why you feel so under the pump.

- Are your days far too busy from squeezing in too much?
- Does it feel like the workload at school is too much to manage?
- Does it feel like you're not getting enough chill time?
- Are you spending most of your non-school time doing schoolwork?
- Does it feel like you're constantly rushing and running out of time?
- Do you try to remember everything you have to do rather than use a diary?
- Are your desk, bag and locker cluttered and messy?
- Do you feel stuck when you think about everything you need to do?
- Do you avoid some classes because you're not up to date?
- Do you find you are comparing yourself to other people who look like they're nailing it?

If you ticked a few boxes there's a possibility you're getting caught in the overwhelm trap.

And if you feel gross and out of sorts, here's why.

Overwhelm shows up when your brain thinks you're under threat. It sees the assignments, tests and homework piling up on your desk, and it panics. Your brain wants to protect you, and so it gives you a big burst of cortisol—the stress-response chemical that makes you stronger and ready to tackle the threat (i.e. the pile of work on your desk).

But as much as your brain is trying to help you, sometimes it can get a bit overprotective and give you too much cortisol, which can make you feel stuck, yuck and out of control.

It can also mess with your thoughts. Here's how.

You think you can't handle everything you need to do. (We know it's not true, but it sure feels like it is.)

You might cry, slam doors, and yell at your parent because they don't understand one little bit.

You have a meltdown on your bed, pack up your homework, and refuse to give it another chance. (You're not alone here.)

And you don't need to be a rocket scientist to work out what happens next. The overwhelm gets worse.

We've all been there, and it's revolting. But don't stress too much. On the following pages I'll share how you can wave goodbye to overwhelm.

5 WAYS to give your brain a break

1. STOP, DROP AND SORT – GIVE YOUR BRAIN A FRESH START

STOP. Hit the stop button on your life. Seriously, you need to do this if you want to stop overwhelm in its tracks.

DROP. Yes, drop everything from catch ups to Netflix time. Free up a big chunk of time. This will save you from spiralling down further than you need to.

SORT. Get your music on, have snacks by your side, and sort what's on your mind.

Take a note out of Adam's book:

> "I was drowning in work and falling behind. I had stuff everywhere, my desk looked like a tip, and my head was all over the shop. My mum was on my case, teachers were sending emails, and things were getting worse.
>
> I made sure I had nothing on. I blocked out Thursday night and Saturday afternoon to get sorted and to get it all done. Best decision I made. I felt heaps better after."

2. GET COMFORTABLE WITH SAYING "NO" – YOU'RE ONLY HUMAN

When you're overwhelmed you may find yourself:

- getting cranky, teary, or short-tempered
- blowing little things into big things so they are way out of proportion
- believing you're not good enough, smart enough, or capable of keeping up with the demands of your school year.

And your overwhelmed mind will trick you into believing this again and again.

Here's the thing. People will still like you if you say "No". Trying to be a people pleaser is a total waste of time. There are almost eight billion people on the planet, and you can't please them all! Where would you start and where would you stop?

Knowing what you can handle is your superpower. Only you know whether your week is too full, you're doing too much, or the fun, calm and chill time you need to be happy and healthy is slowly disappearing from your life.

Follow Xavier's lead:

> "I worked out I couldn't fit everything in—sport, training, homework, family stuff and heaps of socialising. I said "Yes" to it all, but then the pressure came and the fun disappeared. My Head of Year suggested I drop one thing a week to free up some time. I did that, and it made all the difference."

3. DO A BRAIN DUMP – IT TAKES THE PRESSURE OFF

A brain dump helps your brain settle itself, and gives your brain the chance to help you without the weight of overwhelmed thinking.

Dumping your work and tasks helps you make a plan.

Copy Chantelle's approach:

> "I spread all my books, files and notes across my bed. One subject at a time, I randomly wrote everything I needed to do on my whiteboard. I just dumped it, and got it out of my head and onto the board. It felt like a huge weight had lifted off my shoulders. I recommend getting a whiteboard. I use mine heaps."

4. DO A MIRROR CHECK – FIND OUT WHAT YOU NEED

Take a look in the mirror and ask yourself these questions:

- **Do I need help from another person to get started or to keep going?** If the answer is "Yes", ask for it.
- **Do I need an explanation or more information to get started, keep going or finish off?** If the answer is "Yes", go get it.
- **Do I need a routine so I'm not relying on motivation to get started, keep going or finish off?** If the answer is "Yes", create it.

Here's Isabella's idea:

> "As soon as I know exactly where I'm at and what I need to do, I feel clear and heaps lighter and can work out what I need in order to get everything done. It works really well for me."

5. SHARE THE LOAD – PEOPLE LOVE TO HELP IF THEY'RE ASKED

It goes without saying, but I'm going to say it anyway. High school is not a journey you need to complete on your own.

- Meet with your teachers, and follow up with emails.
- Have a meeting with your Head of Year.
- Chat to your school counsellor, sport coach, social worker, psychologist, chaplain or school mentor.
- Talk with your friends.
- Stay connected to your parents, aunties, uncles and grandparents.

Josh agrees:

"There are so many people who want to help you do your best. You just have to ask them. It took me a while to work it out—better late than never. But when I did, the high school thing was so much easier."

5 WAYS to give your brain a plan

1. DO ONE THING AT A TIME – YOUR BRAIN WILL THANK YOU

Your brain doesn't like it when you make it jump all over the place—from messages on your phone to your Spotify playlist, then back to the English question you're finishing before bouncing over to a group chat and back again.

It's dangerous, and will set you up for wasted time and tears.

Your brain is smart, but not that smart. It can't do two tasks at once, and instead switches between the two as quickly as it can. So instead of doing one task well, it ends up doing both tasks poorly.

And the more tasks you try to do at once, the more your brain must switch from one to another, and the worse your results will be.

Back-and-forth learning is far from ideal. Avoid it whenever you can.

Be kind to your brain. Give it one task at a time and you'll notice you make fewer mistakes, get more done, think more clearly and become more productive.

And who doesn't want more of that?

2. MANAGE YOUR MORNING – START YOUR DAY IN THE BEST POSSIBLE WAY

Maybe you like mornings, maybe you don't. You can't cancel them, but you can choose to make the most of them. There's no perfect recipe for managing them, but teenagers tell me these tips work a treat.

1. **TIME – Note it.** How much time do you need to wake up, eat, shower, get dressed and make your bed without rushing and stressing yourself out? Be generous in your calculations.

2. **ALARM - Set it.** Add some extra time in case something pops up unexpectedly and stops you from running on time. Having five to ten minutes in reserve can make a massive difference to your morning.

TIP: DON'T DO THIS

"I'll print that out in the morning before school."

You're pretty much guaranteeing that your printer will fail, run out of ink, or jam itself with dodgy paper. All our worst nightmares happen when we leave things to the very last minute.

3. DO THE SUNDAY SETUP – SET UP YOUR WEEK AND YOU'LL FEEL GREAT

Your school week can get busy. Too much busyness can send you into a messy spin that feels like panic, craziness and chaos all mixed into one. It's not the best combination.

If you'd like to do high school in the best way, try these six 'Spin Less' steps. They'll help you finish tasks on time, feel prepared and be a lot more organised.

1. **BUILD THE HABIT** - Every Sunday, dedicate around 30 minutes to your Spin Less mission. Set a reminder on your phone to help you get into the habit, and do it when you're feeling awake and fresh. (Hint: don't leave this until 8pm on Sunday night.)

2. **MAKE A 'WILL DO' LIST** - Write down everything you need to be at, to do, show up for, take care of and complete between Monday and Friday. It's worth having your diary and timetable handy. (It can be hard work trying to remember everything.)

3. **ORDER IT** – Order your list from most important to least important. Knowing dates and deadlines will help you decide what needs to be done first. This takes practice, but it will be worth it. Don't panic if you stuff up this step in the beginning. With practice you'll get better at it and it will get easier.

4. **CHUNK IT DOWN** – Decide what needs to be done before and after school. Using your ordered list from Step Three and your diary, write down what you need to do on Monday through to Friday so you have an idea of your week ahead.

5. **STICK IT UP** – Place your Spin Less Plan in a stand-out spot in your house where you go to get stuff done. Your workstation is a great place to start, or maybe on the fridge as that seems to be a very popular spot.

6. **CHECK IT OFF** – It feels good to see your list shrink. So take pride in drawing a big fat line through each completed task and switching 'I will do it' to 'I did it'. With each item you put a line through you'll get a nice little dopamine hit. Look out for it because it's very handy when life gets busy and to-do lists get long.

4. DO THE WEDNESDAY WIND UP – SMOOTH YOUR WAY INTO THE WEEKEND

Most high schoolers say they feel exhausted towards the end of the week, which can lead to them taking shortcuts, dodging deadlines, and even showing up half-hearted.

To reduce the chance of your week spinning out of control, make the Wednesday wind up your week-ending power move.

Repeat Steps One to Six from the Sunday setup, but this time focus on Thursday, Friday, Saturday and Sunday. This will help you finish your week reaching for the sky rather than crawling across the finish line.

TIP

Sometimes life throws you curveballs that can stop you from finishing everything on your list. It's okay. Any incomplete tasks from Monday to Wednesday can be added to the new list. If you know you're doing your best to establish your organising habits then you're winning!

5. DO YOUR TWO-HOME SWITCH – IN THE EASIEST POSSIBLE WAY

If you switch homes during the week or on the weekend, your organisation skills are probably already finely tuned and you're ahead of the game. Good on you.

But if you're new to switching and still finding your feet, that's okay. Try these tips to help streamline your switch.

TIPS FOR YOU

1. **DOUBLE UP** – Keep a set of personal essentials in each home.
2. **GRAB-AND-GO BOX** – Find a box to put all the bits and pieces needed at each house. Use them at one house, and then add them to the box so you don't forget them on switch day.
3. **CHECKLIST** – Create a list and check it off the night before you switch. Trying to remember everything is hard work, a checklist takes the pressure off.
4. **REMINDERS** – Alarms and reminders will help you manage your time.
5. **KEEP IT SIMPLE** – Avoid overloading your switch day with extra commitments.

6. **STAY PUT** – While exams are on, you may be better off staying in one home so nothing changes and you can focus on studying. Think about what would work best for you.

7. **SPEAK UP** – Let your teacher know it's switch day, especially if there's extra work coming your way and you know your time is limited.

8. **SHOUT OUT** – Switching can be tiring. Please ask for help when you need it.

TIPS FOR YOU AND YOUR FAMILY

1. Set up a group chat on Messenger or SMS so everyone is in the loop.
2. Use an online shared schedule to keep track of events and key dates.
3. Talk about staying put at one house during a test week.

SECTION 4

HELLO FRIENDSHIP ZONE

Goodbye drama, gossip and judgement

HELLO FRIENDSHIP ZONE

Friends are people who light up your day when you're in their company or messaging each other. You know the ones. They add to your life, boost you up, and have always got your back.

Having solid friendships, especially at school, can make your high school journey much more fun because you're probably like every other teenager. You want to feel safe, fit in and find your happy place, especially at recess and lunchtime breaks.

Do you know what makes a healthy and happy friendship? There are some key signs your friendship is going well. And when it's not going so well, there are some key things you can do to make it better.

SIGNS AND SIGNALS YOUR FRIENDSHIP IS GOING WELL

A friendship will feel right when you have a lot of the below going on. These things may not be happening all the time, because friendships and relationships ebb and flow. But it's worth checking in and making sure your friendship is lifting you up, not dragging you down.

Here are a few signs you're on the right track:

- You have each other's back.
- You can trust each other with important stuff.
- Your friendship feels equal and fair.
- You respect their boundaries, and they respect yours.
- You do things for each other and expect nothing in return.
- You feel accepted and respected.
- You have a nice balance of give and take.
- You can be yourself.
- You have disagreements and down times, but you talk them out and move on.
- You like the way they speak to other people.
- Your friendship gives you both the space you need to have other friends.
- You are kind to each other.

SIGNS AND SIGNALS YOUR FRIENDSHIP IS DRIFTING OR CHANGING

Here are a few signs that a friendship may not be as strong as it previously was:

- You're arguing a lot.
- You don't feel like yourself around them.
- You feel the trust between you isn't so strong.
- You notice you aren't in touch so much anymore.
- You feel like your friend is trying to own you, or block you from other friendships.
- You're competing with each other.
- You notice invitations have stopped.
- You hear put-downs, sarcasm, and fake positivity towards you.
- You hear gossip and you're getting dragged into dramas.
- You have a gut feeling that something isn't right.

TEENAGE TIPS FOR WHEN FRIENDSHIPS DRIFT AND CHANGE

TRY THIS	RATHER THAN THIS
Trust yourself.	Talk only through devices and messages.
Talk to your friend face to face if possible.	Involve and drag other people in the problem. It will make conversations messy.
Is there something *you* can change, rather than expecting your friend to do all the changing?	Try to mould your friend so they are the same as you.
Ask a parent for help.	Focus on their flaws.
Be patient, and don't be too quick to end the friendship.	Ghost them.
Check in and ask if they're okay.	Try to solve issues in front of everyone else in your group during your lunch break.
Be honest.	Point out their past mistakes and friendship stuff-ups.
Be kind.	Talk about them behind their back.
Write a letter or a card.	

Not all friendships last a lifetime. Some last for a couple of months, some for a year, and others for much, much longer. But keep in mind that you and everyone in your year group have one thing in common: you're all trying to find good-fit friendships.

This might mean you and your friend
go your separate ways.

Going your separate ways can hurt your heart,
but it happens from time to time.

You're allowed to outgrow people,
and they're allowed to outgrow you.

Outgrowing a friend doesn't mean you have
permission to behave badly towards them.

And they don't have permission to
behave badly towards you.

If you turn left and they turn right,
leave them be and hope they do the same for you.

Keep your head up and just do you.

Be unstoppable. It suits you.

5 WAYS *to step away from dangerous drama*

1. TRUSTWORTHY – BE IT

If someone shares a secret or edgy information with you, remember that you have been trusted.

And that's a big deal.

But when a secret lands in your hands you might be tempted to let it leak, especially if the details are super exciting and sharing it could bring you a gigantic leap in social status and popularity.

So what should you do? Keep secrets tight or let them leak? Both options have consequences.

- **KEEP SECRETS TIGHT** – You will feel good and believe yourself to be a trustworthy person. Be proud of that.
- **LET SECRETS LEAK** – It will feel exciting and risky as you leak information to others at school. But that excitement will soon turn to regret, and that's not a great feeling.

> "Be a loyal friend. Don't try to be cool to fit in. It's a waste of time."
> – JOEL

> ### SOMETHING TO KEEP IN MIND
> Not all secrets are created equal. If the information disclosed to you feels too heavy, and your gut tells you to tell a trusted adult, please do so. Some secrets are far too big for high schoolers to hold on to.

2. GOSSIPING - AVOID IT

Gossiping about someone or being gossiped about are both gross.

If you involve yourself in gossip you are choosing to feel more popular, stronger, or better about yourself by sharing unkind stories and information about another person.

(That person could be a friend, a teacher, a parent, or anyone else.)

Being gossiped about can leave you feeling hurt, angry, anxious and alone. You might think everyone is talking behind your back, and believing what they're hearing. You can't control it, especially if it's doing the rounds on social media, and so you'd rather stay at home than face the awful gossip at school.

If you're in doubt about whether to share gossip, ask yourself two questions:

1. If I share this information, will it boost someone UP or drag someone DOWN?
2. What will I do with this gossip? Pass it on, or keep it to myself?

> ### WHAT WILL YOU CHOOSE TO DO?
>
> Gossip is gross. Shut the gate on it.
>
> Kindness is free. Sprinkle that stuff everywhere.
>
> Be the reason someone feels like
> they belong at school.

Keep a watchful eye on your thoughts and chats, and the comments you write or read in messages and group chats. Do they include drama-digging words such as 'everyone', 'no-one', 'always', 'never', 'everything', 'all' and 'nothing'? These overly general words are often used to add to problems, stir trouble, and make people, groups and issues seem bigger than they are or need to be.

You'll read more about stories and facts on page 130. And you'll see that drama-digging words often hang out on the 'story side' of life. Which is why you should dodge them wherever possible.

You may have heard drama-digging words in action.

- "No-one wants to be in that group. Everyone is toxic."
- "They never include me in anything."
- "Everyone is talking about him and no-one likes him."
- "You always think you're right about everything."
- "I never get invited to anything at all."
- "They're all talking about her and everyone is avoiding her."
- "No-one is listening to anything he says."
- "It's always those girls. They think they own everything."

As soon as you notice these drama-digging words popping up, shut them down straight away.

> "Be kind. Avoid gossip. It only messes up friendships and causes trouble."
> – JESS

3. MATCHING - LEAVE IT

Your friends might be a perfect match for you. You probably like the same music, sports and movies, and love hanging out together on the weekend. Friends in sync are worth their weight in gold.

But it's also good to have friends and classmates who aren't a perfect match.

Why? Because talking with people whose interests, opinions and family backgrounds are different to yours will help you:

- think outside the box
- step out of your comfort zone
- try new things
- talk about topics you didn't know existed.

> "Don't hide away. Get amongst it. Let people meet you, be social, say hello and smile."
> – REBECCA

4. OWNING – PRACTICE IT

You own you. Yes, you do.

And being the owner of anything, comes with *rights* and *responsibilities*.

You own a surfboard. You have the *right* to ride waves on it, but also the *responsibility* to care for it, use it safely around other people, and store it securely.

You own a dog. You have the *right* to feel safe around it, and the *responsibility* to walk, feed and care for it.

You own a backpack full of school books. It's your *right* to use them to learn. It is also your *responsibility* to look after them and put them back in your backpack so they stay in good condition.

You own yourself and you have the *right* to:

- feel safe, hold your own opinion and speak freely
- be included, welcomed, and hang with people you want to hang with
- be respected and treated equally by everyone at your school
- learn in class without being hassled by anyone around you
- speak to people without gossip, drama or ridicule

- use social media without fear of keyboard warriors, online put-downs, rumour or humiliation
- confidently walk between classes or sit in a group during breaks
- play sport, get involved and stay fit without judgement or comparisons.

Now flip it.

Sitting beside your rights are your responsibilities, which are equally important. These are your duties to yourself, other humans, animals, the land, the planet and the environment.

In high school (and everywhere) you have the *responsibility* to:

- allow others to hold their opinion and speak freely
- include and welcome others, and not get in the way of them hanging with their crew
- respect others and treat everyone equally at your school
- let others learn without hassling them
- say "No" to and block gossip, drama and ridicule
- choose not to be a keyboard warrior on social media by putting people down online or getting involved in rumours or humiliation
- let others walk between classes or sit in a group confidently and without interference from you
- allow others to play sport, get involved and stay fit without your judgement or comparisons.

5. JUDGING - PLUG IT

Judges have their place.

Judges are experts in their field who use their knowledge to score competitors and announce winners.

The judge and jury rule the court and decide whether someone is guilty or not guilty.

But the judgement used to find fault in others can throw fuel on the drama fire, especially at school, across social media and on the sporting field.

Here's something to think about. When you judge another person are you thinking, *you're not like me or my group, so you must be wrong, different or weird?*

High school can be a place where people like to point out anything that isn't 'normal' (whatever 'normal' is).

Judgement adds to drama.

- Judgements are often shared with other people: "Did you see her doing that in English? Who does that? I mean really."
- Judgements are based only on what you see in the moment: "He's always late to school. He should get his act together." (Said without knowing the family issues that contribute to his regular lateness.)

- Judgements involve unhelpful comparisons: "Look at her hair. Who would go out like that?"

Who knows who's wrong and who's right?

The problem is, when we judge others at school we can start worrying that others may be judging us in the same way. It can become a messy worry-judgement loop that generates a huge amount of anxiety.

- What do people think of me when I arrive late? Are they judging me? Probably.
- My hair looks awful today, I can't go to school. Everyone will stare and judge me.

Try replacing judging with accepting. You're doing high school your way, and that's perfectly fine.

And remember that judgement comes with a cost. Not many people want the reputation of being judgemental. If you think it's a habit that's creeping into your life, make the decision to stop.

Leave other people alone and focus on yourself.

Even better, look for the good in others—the parts you admire, adore, and want to talk up rather than talk down.

And what if you're around judgemental people? That's easy. Just zip your lips and don't get involved. By doing this you're starving the judgement of oxygen and choosing not to be a drama-digger. And that's a good thing.

If judgement raises its ugly head in a group chat, you can try these:

- Shut it down: *"It doesn't feel great to talk about her like that."*
- Lead the conversation away from judgement and drama by switching from finding fault to talent spotting. Shine a light on what's awesome rather than what's not: *"She was great in my group today and helped me out."*

But if for whatever reason you can't embrace talent spotting, zip your lips.

By taking these actions you are helping to make your group, school, world and planet a drama-free zone. And you should be proud that you're choosing to do so every single time.

SECTION 5

HELLO COURAGE ZONE

Goodbye worry and anxiety

HELLO COURAGE ZONE

It's your choice ...

If you smile

Your thoughts

Choices you make

What you eat and drink

Your decision to ask for help

To exercise and move your body

How you treat yourself and others

To stand up for what you truly believe in

If you say yes or no to a big challenge in life

How you spend your spare time during the week

The time you go to sleep and wake up in the morning ...

The effort you put in to anything you do, even if you don't enjoy it

How you handle failure, disappointment and setbacks in life

If you choose to use feedback to move yourself forward

Your decision to show up, be involved and participate

The way you talk to yourself as you try to fall asleep

How you love and care for animals big and small

How you use social media across all platforms

The respect you give the beautiful planet

To walk away from all types of drama

The movies you watch on Netflix

The books you read for fun

Your routines and rules

To look for the good

To be a learner

To be kind

To love

Your high school experience depends on many of your day-to-day choices.

NOW LET'S TALK ABOUT ANXIETY ...

Anxiety is an emotion that shows up as worried thoughts in your mind and uncomfortable feelings in your body. It can make you feel like you're so out of control, and can pop up at the most random and inconvenient times:

- getting ready to go to a party
- on the way to basketball
- before morning break
- when you see someone at school
- ordering a hot chocolate in a café
- catching the bus in the morning.

If you feel anxious from time to time, you're not alone. It's completely normal to feel this way—especially at high school, where you're facing challenges and catching curve balls every day of the week.

Anxiety can roll like this.

> You wake up in the morning, open your eyes, yawn, have a stretch ...
>
> ... and then suddenly remember the test you've got on that afternoon.

Boom! Your thoughts dive down to stress town, and your head starts filling with negativity, fear, worry and doubts:

- *I'll fail.*
- *I'm useless.*
- *I don't know what I'm doing.*
- *I'm stupid.*
- *It will be too hard.*
- *I don't want to go to school.*

Your brain, which as I mentioned earlier, is hardwired to protect you, will detect these stressful thoughts and think you're in serious danger.

And this is where things can get messy.

To keep you safe from that test, it will give your body a mighty squirt of cortisol so you feel stronger, faster and more powerful in case you need to:

- run as fast as you can
- stand your ground and fight
- remain completely still, hoping the danger (the test) will pass.

Unfortunately, with cortisol now swirling in your blood and your thoughts hanging around in stress town, you've created the 'perfect storm' for anxiety to swamp your body, heart and head.

Different people experience anxiety in different ways. Here's how you might experience it:

- Your breathing changes, and you suddenly feel out of breath, dizzy and weak.
- There's a sick sensation in your tummy. You may even get stomach cramps and think you're going to vomit.
- Your heart beats so fast in your chest that you start to panic because it actually hurts.
- You feel so overwhelmed that you start to cry, and you can't stop the tears rolling down your face.
- You yell, swear, slam doors, or say words you know you'll regret. (And then your brain, thinking it needs to protect you from the embarrassment that comes next, gives you another unnecessary cortisol squirt that only makes things worse.)

And all because you started thinking about that test.

But don't stress too much. You can change things and reclaim your power so you can get out of bed, eat your breakfast, get dressed, make your way to school and show up for that afternoon test without feeling so anxious.

> Here's how to dial down anxiety in **5 STEPS**

1. BREATHE

Focus on breathing with long, slow, deep breaths. This will send a high-speed message to your brain that you're feeling safer now and it can stop being so overprotective.

If it helps, put your hands on your belly and chest to feel your body rise and fall with each breath. Stick with that for as long as you need. You might like to try visualising your breath gently moving in and out of your lungs. This can be very calming, give you something to focus on and help you to settle yourself.

2. SOOTHE

Have your favourite music playlists ready for when you need soothing sounds or particular music to help with your long deep breathing.

3. THINK

Bring your attention to your thoughts.

This is your chance to practise the five-step THINK technique: CATCH, CHECK, CHOOSE, CHANGE and REPEAT (pages 12 and 13).

Instead of:

- *I'll fail.*
- *I'm useless.*
- *I don't know what I'm doing.*
- *I'm stupid.*
- *It will be too hard.*

Try these thoughts:

- *I'll do my best.*
- *I'm doing okay.*
- *I'll give this my best shot.*
- *I'm enough.*
- *I'll show up and write down what I do know. I'll get through this test. Yes, I will.*

4. RECOVER

Give your brain and body time to recover. Behind the scenes, all that cortisol that was swimming in your body needs to be flushed out. To do that it needs exit points to escape, which appear in the form of energy.

If you don't give cortisol those exit points it can stay in your system, making you feel tense, stressed, tight and on edge for longer than you need to.

To create those exit points you need to move:

- dance
- sing
- jump on the trampoline
- go for a run
- play your guitar
- kick the footy
- shoot goals on your driveway hoop
- get a hug from someone you love
- roll on the floor with your dog
- chase the cat
- ride your bike home in the fresh air.

You will feel lighter, settled, and more in control.

5. REWARD AND REPEAT

Have a chat with yourself. Remind yourself that you're good enough, smart enough, capable enough and awesome enough to show up, plonk your butt on a chair, do a test to the best of your ability, and leave.

Keep it simple.

The moon will glow, and the sun will rise again tomorrow. It always has, and always will.

Practise, practise, practise.

If you're 15 years old now and you live to be 100, breathe a sigh of relief because you've got 85 years to work this out. With practice, you can make this your go-to tactic when facing a test or anything else that causes you to feel anxious or stressed.

INCREASE HIGH VIBES AND GOOD ENERGY

Beyond keeping a lid on anxiety and the effect it has on your days, here are 10 more things you can do to boost your energy levels and bring positive vibes to your days.

1. SMILE YOUR WAY TO A BETTER DAY

The great thing about smiling is that it's free. You also get great vibes from another person when they smile at you. And like yawning, it's contagious.

Smiling sends a message to everyone that you're friendly, and up for getting to know them (or at least having a chat). It's a nice little icebreaker, especially when you're trying to get to know people in your classes.

When you smile, your brain knows it's time to release feel-good chemicals—endorphins to chill out, and dopamine to boost your mood. Which means it's totally possible to smile your way to a better day.

So if you're feeling anxious or upset, smile at yourself in the mirror for 15–30 seconds. It might seem weird at first, but stick with it because your brain is a sucker for a smile. It's a great way to start or reset your day. When you see yourself smile, notice how your energy and attitude starts to shift.

2. RIDE THE ROLLERCOASTER

You'll have days you wish would never end, and days you wish would end faster so you can go to bed, wake up and start over.

Don't expect every day, subject and lesson to be awesome, because that's a little unrealistic.

Instead, expect a mix of:

- up days that go perfectly to plan
- down days that knock your confidence, test your patience, and even make you wonder if you're cut out for this high school thing.

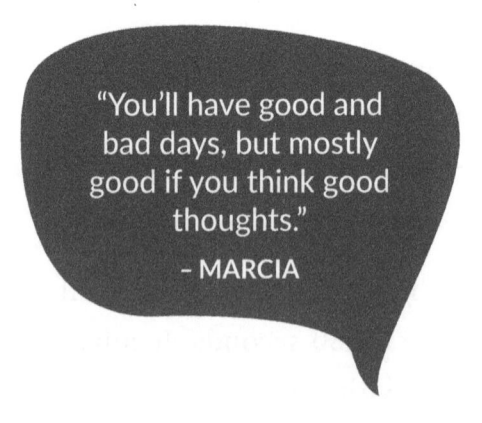

> "You'll have good and bad days, but mostly good if you think good thoughts."
> – MARCIA

3. SAY YES

Opportunities pop up a lot in high school, such as the chance to:

- sign up for an after-school club
- join a team
- sit with people you don't know very well.

Unfortunately, those opportunities can also bring on annoying fears that stop you from saying "Yes", including the fear that:

- you'll look silly
- you won't be liked
- you might fail.

To deal with these fears, you might start coming up with reasons not to get involved. But then it becomes a habit, and you find yourself saying "No" again and again and missing out on heaps of good stuff at school, after school, and with friends.

So start taking big brave breaths and say "Yes". The fear won't disappear completely, but I promise you the joy of joining in and getting involved will be worth it. Feel the fear, and then do the thing you want to do.

4. FOLLOW THE FACTS

FACTS come from the left (logical) side of your brain.

⟹ Non-fiction books contain information that is thought to be true.

STORIES begin in the right (creative) side of your brain.

⟹ Fiction books are filled with made-up and invented tales.

Facts and stories are great. And we need them both to keep school interesting. But high school can get messy if you don't learn to separate them.

And life can get even messier if you tip the balance, forget the facts, and tell yourself too many doom and doubt stories that crush your confidence.

STAY WITH THE FACTS

Fact:	There will be 24 students in the class that starts at 9am today.
Story:	I doubt anyone will ask me to sit with them in class today.
Fact:	My next exam is on March 24.
Story:	I'll never be ready on time, and I'll probably stuff it up anyway.

Fact: The party is fancy dress with the letter T as the theme.

Story: I'll look stupid, and everyone will wonder what I've come as.

Notice how the facts are everything that 'is', and the stories are the made-up bits that trigger emotions such as fear, worry, doubt and anxiety.

> ### THE GOOD NEWS IS YOU HAVE TWO OPTIONS:
> 1. Keep telling yourself anxiety-triggering stories in your mind (not recommended).
> 2. Tell yourself stories that trigger emotions such as hope, pride, joy and love (highly recommended).

Here's how to take advantage of that second option.

Fact: I've got a test on Thursday.

Story: If I finish the practice questions and revise the notes, I should be good to go.

Fact: My team made the grand final.

Story: I can't wait for the game to start. It would be so good if we won.

The stories you tell yourself have tremendous power. And best of all, you have complete control over what those stories are about.

5. SHRINK MOUNTAINS

Problems are a part of life. Problems with friends, homework, sport, tests, and teachers are bound to pop up. But when they do, what will you do?

You could EXPAND the problem. That's where you talk about it so much that it grows and messes with your mind to the point where you feel totally overwhelmed by it and have no idea what to do. (That's so exhausting.)

Or you could SHRINK the problem and keep it in check by following this six-step process.

1. Figure out what the problem is and write it down.
2. Decide whether you need a trusted adult to help you shrink the problem.
3. Think about how you would feel if the problem were smaller or you found a solution.
4. Think of possible ways to shrink the problem. Get your creative mind flowing.
5. Choose an option that feels like the best fit for you.
6. Give it a go, and give it all you've got.

And remember, if your first choice doesn't shrink the problem, choose another option on your list and keep going. Not all problems will shrink out of sight overnight. Some will take more time and persistence. But it's worth it. AND SO ARE YOU.

6. BE YOUR BIGGEST FAN

Wherever you go, there you are.

You are the person you spend the most time with. So it's a good idea to cheer loudly for YOU. Clap like crazy for YOU and speak kindly to YOURSELF. It's not too much to ask, it's free, and available to you 24/7.

Do it. You're worth it.

How? Let's talk about affirmations. These are encouraging thoughts that boost you up and create positive energy within you. They also remind you of your worth, and push you along when you need an encouraging push.

Affirmations come in all shapes and sizes, but the best usually start with one of these:

"I can ..."

"I will ..."

"I am ..."

"I do ..."

"I believe ..."

"I know ..."

How you activate the power of affirmation is up to you. Many teens say they have the most success when they choose a few favourites and use them often. You can swap them out when the time feels right.

How do you make those affirmations stick? You can:

- use them as a screen saver
- write them on your bathroom mirror
- put them on a poster on your bedroom wall
- add them to your workstation whiteboard
- include them in your school diary
- use them in your journal
- put them on your fridge.

Which affirmations should you use? Everyone has their favourites. You'll probably come up with your own, but here are a few to get you started:

- *I can say no.*
- *I am responsible for my own thoughts.*
- *I'm doing my best.*
- *I deserve to be here.*
- *I believe in myself.*
- *I KNOW I'M STILL LEARNING.*

7. WHAT IF?

Two little words.

One tiny question.

'What if?' can be a dangerous troublemaker. But it can also be a first-class power creator.

TROUBLEMAKER

- What if I fail the test?
- What if no-one in the group talks to me?
- What if I look stupid when I show up to training?
- What if I don't make friends?

POWER CREATOR

- What if I give the test my best shot and I surprise myself?
- What if the group are kind and make me feel welcome?
- What if I show up, get involved, and see where that takes me?
- What if I get to know people and we become friends?

> "Look on the bright side. Be careful what you think."
> – ALEXANDER

8. ARE YOU FORECASTING?

You're better off leaving the past behind you. Spending too much time replaying monumental mistakes and stuff-ups in your mind gives you quick access to the 'I've stuffed up before, so I'll stuff up again' club. (A club that's easy to enter but difficult to leave because you get stuck in 'old story' mud that has incredible holding power.)

Remembering and revisiting all your mistakes is exhausting and boring.

High school is better when you're looking ahead.

Learning from the mistakes you made in maths and science, and looking ahead after friendship fallouts, is a much better way to do high school. You're only human after all.

9. THAT QUESTION

"What do you want to do when you leave school?"

You'll probably be asked this question again and again throughout your high school journey.

Teens dread this question, as it can trigger anxiety and drives them crazy.

Maybe you can relate. Perhaps you're thinking:

- I don't know.
- I'm unsure.
- I don't have a clue.
- I might be a teacher, a nurse, or an engineer.
- I thought I knew. But now I have no idea.

If this sounds like you, don't panic. You're in good company with thousands of other teenagers who feel the same way. The truth is, most teenagers haven't worked out what they want to do yet.

And that's okay.

TIPS FROM TEENS JUST LIKE YOU WHO HAVEN'T WORKED IT OUT YET

"Don't stress if your friends know what they want to do. Be patient." – Josh, 17.

"I found there was extra pressure when I had to choose subjects. So I chose subjects I really enjoyed and was interested in. It was the best move I could have made, because I enjoyed them, stayed interested, and got fairly good marks." – Tracey, 18.

"My Head of Year told me to stay curious, keep my eyes open, and notice what I enjoyed doing the most and when I felt like I was in the zone, because that could be a pathway right there. Her advice took heaps of pressure off me." – Justine, 16.

ADVICE FROM YOUNG ADULTS WHO HAVE LEFT SCHOOL AND ARE NOW LOOKING BACK

"Don't choose a job because you're told it pulls in big money. You go to work every day, so it's more important to enjoy what you do rather than earn heaps of cash." – Henry, 25.

"Take as much time as you need to narrow your choices down. In the end you will find the job that is right for you." – Jess, 23.

"Just keep talking, asking questions, reading and watching people at work. I found my pathway accidentally, and now I'm living the dream in the food and fitness industry." – Tahlia, 24.

10. MANAGE YOUR MESSAGES

Be careful.

Messages in text, group chats, Snapchat and online are just words boosted with emojis, videos and funny GIFs. That's all well and good, but if you're one of the millions of teenagers trying to thrive in high school, feel less anxious and enjoy the ride, you also need to be wary of the hidden traps layered in faceless messages.

When you talk to humans face to face you also get:

- facial expressions
- smiles and frowns
- tears and bouts of belly-bursting laughter
- moments of total joy and connection.

It makes sense that humans love to meet face to face with other humans. It helps you feel like you fit, and you get better at communicating and handling surprises both awkward and awesome.

But there's also a risk.

Talking face to face means thinking on your feet. There's no time to edit your words, or back them up with a rainbow or smiling face emoji. There are silences and tricky times when you don't know what to say next. And we can all remember the time we stuffed up and wished the ground would open up and swallow us.

But there's a reward for that risk.

Real friendship happens when there's less guessing, wondering, and trying to work out what was meant in a message or text. Like this :

- I know they've 'seen' the message, but they haven't replied.
- Are they in a hurry and didn't have time to write more?
- Are they upset with me?

Be careful. Without the face-to-face connection, you can miss out on the facts and be left to rely on the story. And we all know how that can end.

Be careful. If you feel anxious, worried or overwhelmed it's easy to overthink messages and jump into a juicy story you know doesn't make sense.

Be careful. Hiding behind a screen is easy, but it can create chaos that makes life harder than it needs to be.

Be smart. If in doubt, call or talk face to face.

SECTION 6

HELLO MVP ZONE

Goodbye crazy comparisons

HELLO MVP ZONE

You are the most valuable player at your school and in your life.

Why? Because you choose how you show up to every class, conversation and moment with your family, friends, mates and teachers.

This chapter gives you 15 tools to help you be more mindful, vibey and positive.

Go on, show up, and be an MVP.

BE MINDFUL,
CHOOSE YOUR VIBE,
AND SHARE POSITIVITY.

BE MINDFUL (MVP)

1. BUILD BOUNDARIES

A boundary is an invisible line you draw for yourself.

The first step towards establishing clear and healthy boundaries is being mindful of what you need to be your best.

BOUNDARIES ARE

- your limits. They help define your personal space, how you spend your time, the way you feel around people, and how you take care of your belongings.
- your rules. They keep you in charge of your mood, your words, your energy and your vibe.
- your signs. They remind you to respect, value and look after yourself.
- your way. They shine through your own words, actions and choices.
- personal. You decide what you keep out and what you let in.
- stable. They stay the same, and don't keep changing to fit each person or group.

BOUNDARIES ARE NOT

- rules that tell other people how to behave
- changing all the time
- a sneaky way to control other people
- a way to be the boss and tell other people what to do.

People like being around people who have clear boundaries. Why? Because there's less mystery, and they know where they stand. When you feel strong and confident you'll find it easier to set boundaries. You won't be so fixated on hoping people like you, and you won't be bothered so much by a sneaky fear of being rejected.

Want to get better at communicating your boundaries?

Here are some phrases you can use:

- "I'm not sure I agree…"
- "I prefer this way…"
- "This is hard for me…"
- "I've thought about it and I think…"
- "I'm feeling uncomfortable…"
- "I would rather not…"
- "It's important that…"
- "It doesn't feel right…"
- "I've decided…"
- "I think we disagree on this…"

Is there an area where you would like to practice building healthy boundaries?

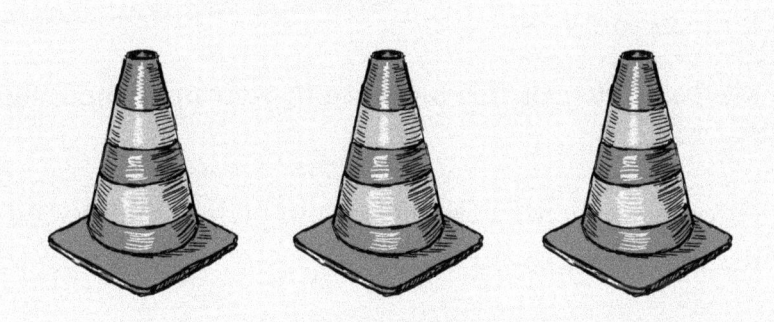

If you know from your head to your toes that something doesn't feel right,
it's easy to be quiet, doubt yourself and slip out of sight.

Trust your boundaries, your beliefs, and your insight.

Stand steady. Show up.

Even if you're shaking or your voice is trembling,
believe in your boundaries. You built them for a reason.

Speak up.

2. SAY "NO"

It's okay to say "No".

Maybe you've got this big voice in your head shouting "No!"

Or perhaps there's a feeling in your belly rumbling and reminding you to say "No."

Or perhaps your heart is beating wildly to the rhythm of "No."

Take notice. You know what's right for you.

And if you get the wobbles because "No" feels hard to say (because everyone is looking at you or everyone else is saying "Yes"), try this: Trust yourself.

3. BE IN YOUR YEAR

It's fair to say that thinking about the past can help you learn and reflect. And looking to the future helps you make plans.

But too much of either isn't great, and can even make you doubt yourself, worry, and feel anxious.

Resist the temptation to zoom forward and think about the years ahead.

Flying into the future can be a dangerous trap for high schoolers. It can crush your confidence and flood you with doubt.

Avoid it.

You have one job. BE IN YOUR YEAR.

> **Give this year your best shot.**
>
> **Tackle it one day at a time.**
>
> **One week at a time.**
>
> **One month, term and semester at a time.**
>
> **And once you're done with this year, <u>then</u> you can think ahead to the next.**

No-one was born an expert at anything. Every musician, athlete and high school student started at the beginning. They didn't know everything, and probably struggled and made a lot of mistakes along the way.

Give yourself permission to be exactly where you are. Each year will have its challenges and its triumphs. Some years will be better than others. That's normal and to be expected. Be prepared to feel nervous, stressed, proud and excited all at the same time.

Gear yourself up to having no idea what's going on in some subjects, and prepare yourself for the exact opposite—feeling like you're totally smashing it, and the subject could be easy.

Be an unstoppable high schooler. It suits you.

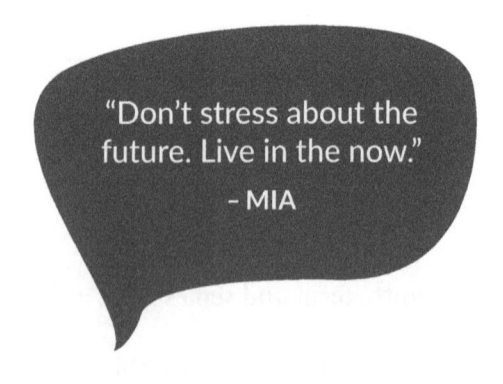

> "Don't stress about the future. Live in the now."
> – MIA

4. CHILL OUT TO CHARGE UP

Choosing to chill out is the best gift you can give yourself. And it's one that keeps on giving.

Looking after you means you're also setting a boundary like this—*I am important and to keep showing up as an MVP on my high school journey, I need to make sure I look after me.*

And with this in mind, you can get busy coming up with 'wind down to charge up' options.

Here are some ideas teens have shared with me for chilling out to charge up.

- "Play sport, exercise, and move. I find I handle my day more calmly if I exercise regularly and it's a good break from school's routine."
- "I hang with my mates after my game. We watch the next team play and chill out for a couple of hours together."
- "I have a bath every Sunday night, and I also have clean sheets on my bed. Bliss."
- "A Netflix session does it for me."
- "I cook with my sister. We listen to music and make healthy snacks for the week ahead."
- "I play basketball on the driveway with my mum or dad."
- "Reading in the hammock with my dog is my thing."
- "I surf. Nothing in the world is better than surfing."

- "An early night or sleeping in always works for me."
- "I walk the dog. It's even better if it's on the beach."

Did you notice that some of their wind downs were more active than others? That's because we're all different, and so we wind down differently.

- If you wind down by lying on the couch watching Netflix, be mindful of that and do it.
- If you wind down by riding your bike along the coast and then stopping to get an ice cream, that's totally fine too.

Did you notice that some examples involved being with people while others were more 'being alone' type activities?

- If you're more introverted, you may prefer to wind down on your own and in a more peaceful way.
- On the flipside, if your personality is more extroverted then you might be drawn to doing high-energy activities with other people.

How you wind down isn't too important. What is important is that you're making the choice to wind down.

Failure to wind down can have serious consequences. It's worth paying attention to how your thoughts, emotions, and behaviour change when you're not charged up enough. You probably become cranky, impatient and rude. You may even become emotional, teary and tired.

But wait. There's more. Overthinking, anxiety and excessive worry can also show up to spoil your day. (This explains why teenagers aren't big fans of this troublesome trio.)

If you want to stay charged up so you're ready to concentrate, participate and learn at school, making time to wind down is absolutely essential. Just do it.

5. TUNE IN TO YOU

Be mindful by tuning in to the voice in your head that only you can hear.

Listen to your voice of reason reminding you to trust your gut. There's no logical explanation for it, and it's hard to put into words. But you know when something feels right or doesn't feel right. Go with that.

No-one has more right to be at your school than you. Believe that.

Get involved. Show up, join in, and have a go—even if fear is tempting you to say "No".

Expect gaps in your knowledge. It's impossible to know what you haven't learnt.

Find a reason to go towards a challenge rather than run from it. You'll get a mighty dopamine boost too.

CHOOSE YOUR VIBE (MVP)

1. FIND YOUR FLOW

Try not to:

- expect everyone in high school to think the same way you do. (That would be rather boring.)
- believe you know everything about everything. (You'll make yourself unteachable.)
- think you're always right. (That would mean other people are always wrong.)
- confuse 'hard' with 'new'. (Just because you've never done it before doesn't mean it's hard or impossible.)
- spend too much time with people who talk about everything they don't like about high school. (It can be contagious and get you down.)

Find your own flow. Walk to the beat of your own drum.

> "Show up with a good attitude. It makes a big difference."
> – HAYDEN

2. BE INTERESTED

It's hard work trying to be interesting to everyone around you. Believing people will like you more if you have a story to tell or a funny joke to share might make you feel nervous and/or anxious.

It's easier and more natural to be interested in the people around you. There's a bonus too—you'll feel far less anxious because you're not trying to be someone you're not.

Being interested starts with:

- listening to others when they are talking (without thinking what you will say next).
- asking a question. (Questions get easier when you listen well.)
- laughing with friends. (That's a good feeling.)
- practising being okay with moments of silence. (You don't have to fill every quiet gap.)

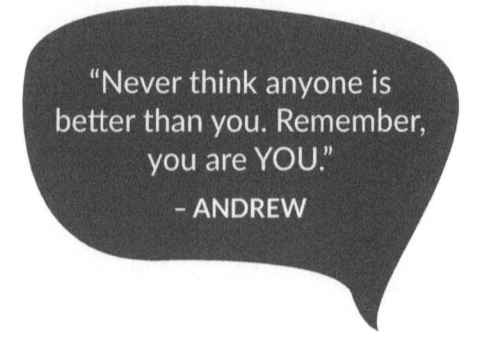

> "Never think anyone is better than you. Remember, you are YOU."
> – ANDREW

3. SIBLINGS AND SUPERSTARS

During your high school journey, your sister, stepbrother, or cousin may have a reputation that isn't great. And you might feel like you're being unfairly judged because you're related. You might be worried everyone thinks you're the same.

In this situation there are two great ways you can build your own identity at school.

1. **TAKE A CHANCE** – Be proud. Show up with your own style and energy. Focus on your schoolwork, and choose friends who help you shine and find your own groove. Teachers and other students will see this quick-smart. They might know you're related, but will also see you for you and be able to set you apart.

2. **ACCEPT THE CHALLENGE** – Stay strong. If you hear complaints about your sibling that upset or embarrass you, hold your head high and keep making the best decisions for you. It's not always easy, and maybe you wish things were different. And they might be one day. But right now you need to remind yourself that as much as you love and support your brother, cousin or stepsister, you can't control what they choose to do. You can only control you. So do that.

But what if your sibling is a superstar? What if your brother, sister, stepbrother, or stepsister started school ahead of you and carved their name into the school's history books? What if your surname rings bells of excitement for teachers? They'll be curious to know whether you have the same academic, leadership or sporting talent as your older sibling.

You might hear:

- *"Your brother is the best footballer. Do you play footy too?"*
- *"Your sister played the leading role in the drama production last year. Do you have the same talent?"*

Here's the deal. Since the beginning of time, people have been comparing one thing to another, including brothers and sisters. It's only natural. But if you find yourself feeling frustrated and you're over it, try this three-step process:

1. Smile, and let them sing your sibling's praises. It's great to see other people do well.
2. Remind yourself that your sibling's strength is not your weakness. You are not them, and they are not you.
3. Try not to feel offended, jealous or upset. You have your own talents and interests.

4. LOVE YOUR LOCKER

Think of your locker as a tiny version of your bedroom and workstation. If it's sorted, you'll feel sorted. It's that simple.

10 WAYS TO MAKE YOUR LOCKER WORK FOR YOU:

1. **LOCK IT** – Keep it safe. Don't share your combo or your key.
2. **TIMETABLE** – Have it on display loud and clear.
3. **MAGNETIC CLIPS AND HOLDERS** – Use them for all the little bits and pieces.
4. **HOOKS AND CLIPS** – Hang things up and keep it neat.
5. **WHITEBOARD ON THE INSIDE** – Add reminders to keep you on track.
6. **NOSE TEST** – Keep it clean, and remove all food and clothes each day.
7. **FILE HOLDERS** – Make sure your books are kept upright with the spines in sight.
8. **STORAGE** – Store more in your locker, and less in your bag.
9. **KIND WORDS** – Stick happy notes inside, such as "You've got this!"
10. **QUIET TIMES** – Visit your locker during less busy times. Not having to hustle through a jam-packed locker area will help you stay calm on busy days.

5. HANDLE HOT DESKS

Many high school classes use 'hot-desking'. You walk in, find a desk, and make it your own. And then do it all over again when you get to your next class.

You might love it, dislike it, or not care either way.

If you're a disliker, it may be because you feel a little lost. You might prefer to have your own personal and familiar space, like you did in primary school or at home at your workstation.

Warning: you can feel a lot more anxious and nervous if you think too many worrying thoughts about hot-desking:

- Will my favourite desk be taken?
- Will everyone be looking at me when I walk in?
- Will I be separated from all my friends and have to sit alone?

High schoolers shared their best hot-desking tips with me:

- "You get used to it. And everyone is in the same boat."
- "After a while you get comfy in the class, and where you sit is not so important."
- "You get to mix things up and meet more people in your year."

SHARE POSITIVITY (MVP)

1. CHOOSE KINDNESS

Kindness is a choice.

Don't wait for others to show kindness first.

You go first.

Be kind, lead the way, and I guarantee people will follow.

Humans love to show kindness, receive it, and see acts of kindness happening all around them.

It's your choice to show kindness to:

- yourself
- your brothers, sisters and parents
- your friends
- your classmates
- younger and older students
- people at school you've never met but walk past every day
- teachers
- gardeners
- bus drivers
- the planet, environment and animals big and small.

Kindness comes with ZERO expectation that you'll get something in return.

KINDNESS TO YOU

Think kind thoughts about yourself.

Forgive yourself when you stuff up.

Give yourself chill time when you need it.

Get enough sleep.

Eat mood-boosting food.

Move your body in your favourite way.

Read awesome books.

Listen to great music and podcasts.

Enjoy unplug time.

Spend time outdoors in fresh air.

Hang out with humans.

Laugh until your belly hurts.

Show respect.

KINDNESS TO FRIENDS AND STUDENTS AT SCHOOL

Invite another person to join in.

Include a friend in a group chat.

Choose to include rather than exclude.

Make a birthday cake.

Slide a happy message into a locker.

Offer to help a friend who finds a subject tricky.

Compliment a classmate on their success.

Say "Hello".

Say "Thank you".

Share an umbrella between classes.

Wait for someone after class.

Show respect.

KINDNESS TO TEACHERS AND ALL SCHOOL STAFF

Offer to help when you can see it's needed.

Say "Thank you".

Send an email of appreciation.

Ask "How are you?"

Tell a teacher how they have helped you.

Offer to carry a heavy load.

Say "Happy birthday".

Talk about staff positively.

Hold a door open for someone so they can go first.

Compliment a teacher.

Give thanks for the garden and school grounds.

Acknowledge teacher talent.

Show respect.

KINDNESS TO PARENTS, FAMILY AND PETS

Make a cuppa.

Cook a meal and clean up afterwards.

Say "Thank you".

Hug and show affection.

Spend time together.

Thank them for the things they do for you.

Take your dog for a walk.

Tell them you appreciate them.

Send a text or "Love you" message.

Keep them in the loop and up to date.

Leave a note.

Keep connected on your switch week.

Show respect.

2. GROW AN ATTITUDE OF GRATITUDE

Have you heard of a bucket list? It's an exciting wishlist of things you're busting to do and see in your lifetime.

It's awesome to look forward to fun stuff—keep doing it. But have you noticed how easy it is to focus on what you want to have rather than what you already have in your life right now?

> **Being grateful isn't comparing yourself to anyone else. It's paying attention to the positives in your life, appreciating what you do have, and focusing on what is working well at school.**

Gratitude, like kindness, is FREE, available to you 24/7, and it's one of the easiest ways to feel more peaceful, happy and settled at school.

Your brain likes grateful thinking so much that it gives you a juicy hit of dopamine (there it is again, the brain's reward chemical) to remind you to keep thinking in grateful ways.

High school can be tricky sometimes. So if you want to reduce pop-up feelings of stress, worry and anxiety, add grateful thoughts at every opportunity:

- **Walking from class to class:** What can you be grateful for right now? Friends walking with you? Rainbow in the sky above? Your warm jacket? The smile on the face of your teacher when you arrive?

- **Being with your friends during breaks:** What can you be thankful for? The fact that you've found your crew? Laughter and funny jokes? Shooting hoops? The abundance of books and technology in the library?

- **Preparing for exams and tests:** What can you appreciate? Help from teachers who reply to your emails and help you when you need it most? Your workstation, data allowance and access to the internet? Your dog curled up at your feet?

- **Getting on the bus at the end of the day:** What can you appreciate in this moment? Chill out time after a busy day? Chatting with friends or listening to music? Relaxing while the bus driver gets you home safely?

If you'd like to grow your gratitude attitude, a journal is a great way to start.

Each night before you go to bed, jot down a few things you're grateful for. You'll think less about any worries in your life and more about the positives.

Here are some grateful thoughts your fellow teens have shared with me:

- *"The food at the canteen is great, and we can order online."*
- *"Laughing with my besties."*
- *"I don't get wet between classes because the path is under cover."*
- *"Playing sport after school. It's the best part of my day."*
- *"I can catch the bus to and from school."*
- *"The drama centre at school is the best."*
- *"My science teacher is super helpful, and explains everything if I ask."*
- *"Music plays at recess and lunchtime, and we get to choose the playlists."*
- *"Interesting speakers come and talk about their jobs and careers."*
- *"The chill-out area is so good."*
- *"I love the school chapel. It's so quiet in there."*
- *"The technology options are amazing here."*
- *"Movies are on in the library when it rains."*

Do you feel like giving gratitude journaling a go?

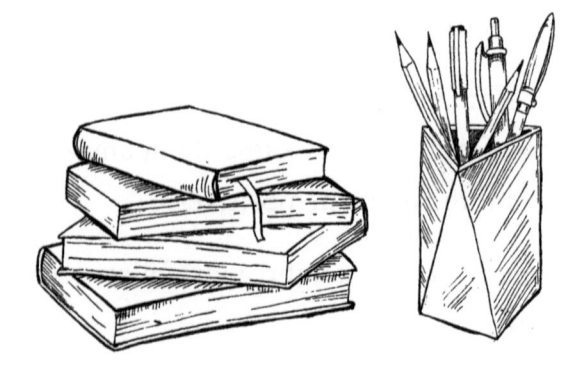

If you're tempted, here are some helpful prompts to get you started:

- What did you participate in today that you appreciated?
- Did a new opportunity come your way?
- Did a friend do or say something that made a difference to you?
- Did a teacher help you out or spent time with you?
- Was there something in nature that you loved?
- Was there a skill or concept that you learned?
- Is there something you own or borrowed that made your life easier?
- Is there someone in your life you are thankful for?
- Do you have a skill, ability or talent that you're thankful for?
- How good are your family, your pets, a hot shower and a comfy bed?

3. COUNT YOUR WINS

In your life there's so much to be proud of. Be mindful of that. Small achievements are a big deal because they all add up.

Take notice when you:

- answer a question correctly in maths
- sign up to the debating club
- complete a challenge in science you thought was way beyond your reach.

These moments matter. They boost your mood, and remind you how well you're doing in and out of school.

> **TIP**
>
> Write your 'fist pump' moments in a journal or a file on your phone. It is a great way to give yourself a lift when you're feeling flat or your confidence has taken a hit.

Celebrating small wins is better than stressing over small worries. Like this:

- If you don't love public speaking, be proud that you did your three-minute talk in front of your English class. You did that.
- Perhaps running isn't your thing. Acknowledge the fact that you completed the entire cross-country course and ran your personal best. You did that too.

It's not about being the best, coming first, or taking home the shiny medal. It's about choosing to show up, giving it your best shot, and giving yourself a pat on the back for your own moments of success.

Don't be sidetracked by the success of others. Let them count the precious wins that are important to them. Like you, they have the right to do that.

4. CATCH COMPARISONS

Comparing yourself to other people is normal. It can motivate you, and even remind you what you have to be grateful for.

It can also send you into a crazy competitive spin that steals joy from your life.

There will be people at your school who have a stand-out talent or lots of luck. But instead of feeling envious or jealous, or having thankless thoughts, be the person who admires them, supports them, and cheers loudly as they run their own race. It's the best way to celebrate and show the world your mindset of kindness and grace.

Instead of putting yourself down with thoughts of 'lack' and 'less', be the person who stands up for you, your talents and your personal best.

Beware of the comparison trap. It can trick you into believing you're not fast enough, tall enough, skinny enough, funny enough, smart enough or good enough.

Whisper these words:

> *Their talent is not my weakness. I am good enough.*
> (There's an awesome affirmation in action.)

5. LEAD YOURSELF

High school offers loads of chances to nominate yourself for a leadership position:

- Sport Crew
- Drama Club
- Environment Group
- Year Captain
- Technology Team

But what if you have never had a leadership role? Or you were a leader and didn't like being in that position?

Here's the thing. Leadership starts with you practising six habits:

1. Be truly interested in the position you nominate for. Fakes get found out.
2. Don't try to be perfect. You will exhaust yourself being someone you're not.
3. Listen to other people and their ideas. People like to be heard.
4. Show up on time. It's polite and a good habit to build.
5. Say what you think is right. Speak your opinion respectfully.
6. Keep your word. Do what you say you're going to do.

Lead yourself well, practise these six habits often, and you'll soon find out whether leadership positions are for you.

SECTION 7

HELLO SUCCESS ZONE

Goodbye unhelpful habits

HELLO SUCCESS ZONE

Daily habits are your best friend in high school, and it's never too late to introduce them into your life. Here are five habits that will ensure you're not just getting through each day in high school. They will set you up to THRIVE.

Let's get started. Choose your vibe.

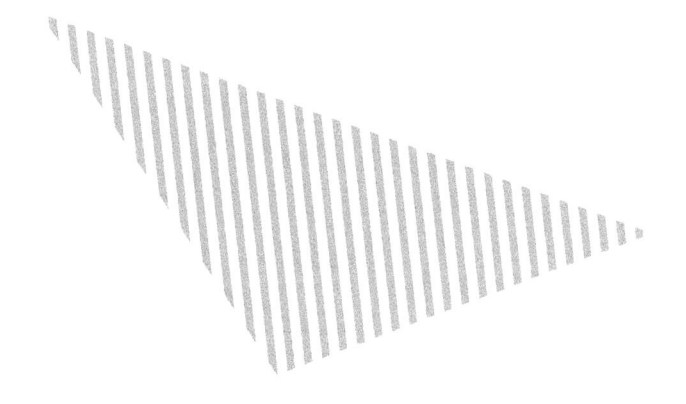

1. CHOOSE YOUR VIBE – GET ACROSS IT

You choose the vibe you bring to everything at school—subjects, assemblies, homework, sports days, classes, buses, tests, timetables, teachers, groups, friends, even your school uniform and devices.

And that means your

- thoughts, ideas, opinions, mindset and decisions
- facial expressions and body language
- energy, feelings and emotions
- words, actions and behaviours

are your responsibility.

2. HANG WITH HUMANS – GET AMONGST IT

Don't confuse being social with being popular. They're not the same thing.

Hanging with humans in real life means getting involved at school and in clubs, teams and your community.

Humans are designed to hang with humans who share similar interests. How you do this is up to you. Your personality may lead you towards socialising at parties or with groups of people. Perhaps you prefer walking with a friend, being a member of a community group, or speaking on the phone. How you decide to be social doesn't matter so much. It's the fact you're being social that really matters most.

You increase your chances of meeting people who you may become friends with when you get amongst it rather than spending most of your time at home, in your bedroom or on a device.

Yes, there may be times when you want to be alone. But if you're feeling a bit out of the loop, lonely or disconnected, go where the humans are.

⬆ MORE OF THIS	LESS OF THIS ⬇
Adding your name to the lunchtime club	Only communicating through a device
Joining the team	Doing too much on your own
Saying "Yes" if you're invited	Avoiding anything new
Sitting with people at lunch	Hiding away at lunchtime
Volunteering	Waiting to see what's in it for you
Offering to help	Keeping to yourself
Allowing time to talk at the lockers	Rushing and being back-to-back busy
Suggesting a catchup	Always waiting to be invited

3. AIM FOR ACTIVE – GET ONTO IT

You'll feel fitter, healthier and you'll sleep better when you move your body every day. Moving your body also helps you cope with the ups and downs of tests, teachers, subjects, socialising, and how you feel about yourself every day of the week.

Why? Because when your body is moving your brain rewards it with a big fat dose of endorphins—the 'happy' hormones that boost your mood and your confidence.

And as a bonus, your thinking improves after physical activity because your brain gets more oxygen.

But if you're not the team-sport type, don't stress. You can still enjoy the benefits of being active. There are so many 'active' options waiting to be added to your day.

If you've got a dog, walk it and get some vitamin D at the same time. (Another great natural and easy mood booster).

- Jog, swim, hike, or jump on the trampoline
- Get off the couch and get on your bike
- Bend your body at yoga, or get strong in the gym

- Dance or cruise on your skateboard
- If there are waves in the ocean, get on them.

Psst.

If you're looking for ways to avoid exercise, here are some wise words from high schoolers just like you:

"Playing sport takes my stress away and gives me a break from schoolwork." – Aiden

"I'm not a great swimmer, but I do laps at the pool twice a week." – Shanae

"I've met heaps of people playing basketball. That's a bonus." – Isaac

"Exercising with my friends is heaps of fun, and we're getting fitter." – Alisha

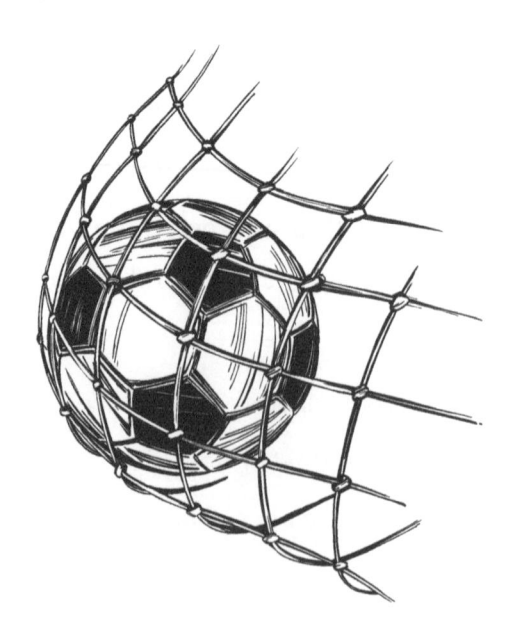

4. EAT MOOD-BOOSTING FOOD – GET AROUND IT

Food, glorious food.

You're smart. You know how you feel when you eat different foods.

Have you noticed you feel better when you eat better and keep your water nearby? Your energy, attitude and motivation are probably up.

Now flip it.

Have you noticed how blah and meh you feel when you eat certain foods and drink less water? Your routine collapses, the couch becomes your best friend, and your schoolwork waits patiently to be completed.

Balance it.

Listen to your body. It's not about being a perfect human who never enjoys chocolate, chips or soft drink. It's about giving your brain and body what they need for you to be awesome.

Do that.

5. BE SLEEP SMART – GET ENOUGH OF IT

Your brain and body need to STOP, be STILL, and SLEEP for eight to ten hours a day.

Why?

As you sleep your brain gets a chance to rest. And you wake up feeling recharged and ready to handle the demands of high school.

What happens when you don't get enough sleep? It shows up like this:

- You can't be bothered doing much (which looks like you're lazy).
- You become moody, cranky or super sensitive (which makes you sound like a joy thief).
- You become anxious and emotional (which makes you feel sad).
- You make more mistakes and have trouble thinking straight (which makes you think and believe you're useless).

To make sure you're getting enough sleep, you need to do more of this:

- Step away from technology at least an hour before you need to sleep. Your brain needs this time to release melatonin (the hormone needed for sleep).
- Set a time to go to bed. Your brain appreciates helpful habits during the week.
- Say "No" to having devices in your room at night. Every buzz and bing will break your deep sleep.
- Say "Yes" to chill out time. Soak in a bath or read a chapter of your book before bed.
- Ease up on the food and drinks close to bedtime. You want to settle your digestive system, not ramp it up.

BE STRONG

Checking your messages one last time will mess with your head and undo your good work. *Don't be tempted.*

BE PATIENT

Give yourself a few weeks to make your new routine a regular routine. *Don't give up too soon.*

BE PROUD

Every night you nail this, you should be really proud of yourself and your choices.

TO STAY IN THE HIGH SCHOOL SUCCESS ZONE, REMEMBER YOU CAN

start on time or start a little late

be certain or feel unsure

try your hardest and fail

nail your first attempt or your 10th

be in a team or go solo

go fast and charge ahead,
or plod along at a slower pace

be loud or quiet

and *still* succeed in high school.

THERE'S NO RULE BOOK OR PERFECT FORMULA FOR HIGH SCHOOL SUCCESS.

CONCLUSION

When you're out and about, look up to the sky.

From time to time you'll notice flocks of birds flying in a beautiful V formation.

What you may not realise is that you and your high school journey have a lot in common with those birds.

- They're on a long and important journey, navigating a migration path that crosses different time zones and climates.
- They're smart and savvy, finding ways to make flying easier for the entire flock as well as their own bodies, wings and hearts.
- They know that by flying together they can save energy and get to their destination safely.

Like a bird on a long flight, you now have the essential tools and tips at your fingertips to look after yourself across the different high school zones and set yourself up for the best high school ride possible.

As you explore the zones and read the words and advice from me and people your age, you'll realise you're not alone. And you can benefit from the journey made by those who have gone before you, as this book will also have answers to questions you may not have thought of or known who to ask.

Now it's your time to show up and say "Hello" to high school with your best energy, enthusiasm and positivity.

In the same way birds find their flying 'sweet spot', I hope using all seven zones in this book and the 85 tips, tools and strategies it contains will help you find your high school 'sweet spot' too.

ACKNOWLEDGEMENTS

So many people of all ages have been involved in this book. Whether it be a quick chat, a deep debate or a rich coaching conversation with a teenager in my office, we can never underestimate the power of sharing, talking and being life-long learners.

To every teenager I have the privilege of coaching, thank you for being brave and asking the questions that are now answered in this book. You have paved the way for teenagers following behind and I'm sure they will be grateful to you for that.

Thank you to my husband, Justin, you are the steady one who always has my back, holds space for my extreme daydreaming ways and reminds me of the importance and impact of my work. I appreciate you and the life we have together.

My son, Caiden, you're the most caring, kind and emotionally intelligent person I know. I'm so proud to be your mum and I'm incredibly grateful we have such a fantastic relationship. You are one of a kind matey and I love you heaps!

Thank you to every educator, school, college and event organiser who invites me to speak to audiences of teens, parents and adults; your commitment to the mental, emotional and social fitness of young people is brilliant.

My sincere thanks goes to schools and organisations who have embraced my work and bulk ordered books so every young person, parent and teacher is reading and sharing the same messages about resilience, optimism and confidence across all high school zones. This is such a game-changer for which I am humbled by and grateful for.

My kind social media community who come from all around the world and mirror my passion for youth and have shared in my book writing journey. I appreciate you and the time you take out of your busy lives to share and support my work.

To every parent who enthusiastically hands a copy of *ROC and RISE* or *Hello High School* to your teenager, and in doing so giving them the HOW-to they've been looking for which is worth its weight in gold. One day they will thank you.

Thank you to my book team, who have helped bring this book from my mind to reality.

Kelly Exeter, my editor who gets my vision and works tirelessly to make sure my ideas and message are delivered in the best possible way. Your expertise is second to none and I'm so glad you are on my team with each book I write.

Bill Harper, thank you for helping my words flow freely and Kym Campradt, once again your attention to detail is greatly appreciated.

My mum, Heather, you are such a great support and encourager of absolutely everything I do. I look forward to our coffee catch ups and great chats. Thank you for being you.

My adorable friends who have been patient in my absence while I write for months. Your messages and encouragement along the way help more than you know.

Most of this book was written early in the morning with Harry my cocker spaniel at my feet. I have enormous appreciation for Harry, 4am writing in a silent house while everyone sleeps and seeing the sensational sun rise so differently each day.

Finally, Maltesers on my desk. When I was writing for days you were there when I needed you the most!

ABOUT THE AUTHOR

Claire Eaton is a proud parent, wife, youth coach, ROC Mindset speaker and author who lives in Perth, Western Australia.

Claire's career working with young people spans over 25 years as an educator, deputy principal, university tutor, youth mentor and mindset coach of young people and parents in her private coaching practice.

Hello High School is Claire's second book, following *ROC and RISE*, the hugely popular book guiding teenagers to build the resilience, optimism and confidence needed to level up at school, in relationships and life.

Claire's practical approach to prevention-based mental, emotional and social fitness of young people is highly sought after, enabling her strong connection with teens, parents and teachers in schools, seminars and mental health events. Claire is incredibly grateful for the endless opportunities she has working with teenagers as they navigate the ups and downs of life.

You can find out more at *ClaireEaton.com.au*